Damien

Also from J. Kenner

Damien

A Stark Novel
By J. Kenner

EVIL EYE

CONCEPTS

Damien
A Stark Novel
By J. Kenner

Copyright 2019 Julie Kenner
ISBN: 9781948050777

Published by Evil Eye Concepts, Incorporated

This is a work of fiction. Names, places, characters and incidents are the product of the author's imagination and are fictitious. Any resemblance to actual persons, living or dead, events or establishments is solely coincidental.

Acknowledgments from the Author

To all the readers who've fallen for Damien Stark over the years, thank you, and enjoy!

Sign up for the 1001 Dark Nights Newsletter
and be entered to win a Tiffany Lock necklace.

There's a contest every quarter!

Go to www.1001DarkNights.com to subscribe.

As a bonus, all subscribers can download
FIVE FREE exclusive books!

Chapter One

They surrounded him. Their lips glossy, their evening dresses tight. Curvaceous bodies, coiffed hair, manicured nails, painted faces. He was drowning in a sea of stunning women, and not one had the power to save him.

Save him?

Where the hell had that come from? He was twenty-four years old, already a sports legend with his name on goddamn cereal boxes, and fast on his way to becoming one of the wealthiest entrepreneurs in the country. *Country?* Fuck that, he was shooting for the world.

Ambitious, maybe. But he'd never thought of ambition as a dirty word. On the contrary, it was what kept him alive. Like the air he breathed, the food he ate. Competition, too. The salty, almost bitter taste of it. The euphoria of success. The dark pit of failure.

He'd learned early how much strength was needed to pull himself out of the pit. More than that, he'd learned how much sacrifice—how much sweat and blood—was required to tame the beast.

And, yeah, maybe he was fucked up. Considering the life he'd led—the past he'd survived—it would be a miracle if he wasn't. But he'd learned a long time ago that the only one who could save him was himself. And he was doing just fine on that score, thank you very much.

And yet, there was that woman...

Frowning, he scanned the room one more time, his gaze lingering on every conversational cluster. Every group surrounding a bar. Every guest hesitating over the buffet table. As the celebrity judge for the Miss Tri-County Texas Pageant, he was expected to make an appearance at events such as this. But it wasn't etiquette that had brought him here. He'd come to the mid-pageant reception for a singular, selfish reason. To find the blond whose presence on stage had stolen his breath and whose words in her interview had touched his soul.

Nichole Fairchild.

She'd spoken of ambition and education. Of science and skill. There was nothing canned in her words. Nothing designed to impress. Nothing fake or false or manipulative.

She'd stood on that stage in her pale blue evening gown, and he'd thought she was the most alive woman he'd ever seen.

And now he'd lost her even before he'd—

"You're Damien Stark!"

At the sound of his name, he turned, his body responding to the wish even though his mind knew that the voice didn't belong to her. Instead, the speaker was a slender redhead sporting a seductive smile. He'd seen her on the stage earlier in the pageant. And damned if he could remember a single detail about her.

"It's so amazing to meet you in person." She stepped closer, so that Damien caught the hint of bergamot in her perfume. "I'm Delancy. I've been a fan since you won your first match. I mean, you're the reason I started watching tennis at all. And now. Your business career. I mean, like wow, right? I read that profile in *People Magazine*. So impressive, but I wasn't surprised by your success. Not at all. I could always tell that there was so much more to you than being an athlete."

"I'm glad you think so." He smiled politely, wondering at her definition of *so much more*. As far as he recalled, that particular article had featured three photos of him on the court, another of him pulling up to an event in a 1969 Jaguar Type E, and a two-hundred word sidebar explaining that he'd rebuilt the car himself in his scarce spare time. There'd also been a reference to his rapidly increasing net worth. They'd called him a money machine, with absolutely no reference to the actual work he did to make the machine hum.

"It's just...well..." She raked her gaze over him, slowing when she dipped below his belt. "You're so much more...*impressive*...in person." Boldly, she met his eyes, hers flush with the kind of silent invitation that had long ago become routine—and which Damien routinely refused.

Not that he was a monk. God forbid. But as far as he was concerned there were only two reasons to have a woman in his bed. Entertainment or escape. And he didn't see this woman providing either.

Besides, he'd come to Dallas with Carmela D'Amato, his most recent entertainment. And he was quite certain that the stunning Italian cover model wasn't the type who would share a man with another woman.

"I appreciate the compliment," he said, holding his ground as the redhead took a single step toward him. "But I'm going to have to decline your kind invitation."

Her mouth opened as the heat faded into panic. "Oh, no, I wasn't—"

"You were, and it's fine. I'm flattered. But no."

This time when she bit her lip, there was nothing seductive about it. "You won't tell—"

"Your secret's safe with me." The pageant rules were strict, and though she hadn't overtly crossed a line, it was clear that all he'd had to do was crook his finger to have her not just breaking the rules but completely decimating them. "But be careful, Delancy," he added with a hint of a smile. "And try to be good."

He left her staring after him as he started across the room toward the exit. The reception was being held in the green room, which also happened to be the smallest ballroom in one of Dallas's finest hotels. Damien had a suite, and since he'd done his duty by making the circuit, that's where he was headed now for a fast fuck to take the edge off. And, of course, to keep Carmela from complaining about the hours she was spending alone, dropping her most recent modeling fee at Northpark Mall.

After that, he'd review the schematics that damn well better have hit his in-box by then. He had an exhibition game in the morning and the conclusion of the pageant in the afternoon. With the two-hour time difference, his Los Angeles team would hate him for scheduling a conference call before the game, but he hired good people and paid them well. They'd deal. And once they'd put the final tweaks on the prototype … well, that would be one hell of a good day for everyone.

He checked his watch and picked up his pace. The evening was getting away from him. At least he knew that Carmela wouldn't mind ordering room service.

And then he saw her.

He'd stopped looking. Had assumed she'd simply stayed in her room. But there she was, the most stunning woman at the reception, and not because she was the most beautiful. Oh, she was pretty, no question there. He could have stood there all night, simply getting lost in the sensuality she projected, getting burned by the heat of her.

But she wasn't a classic beauty. More like the homecoming queen. Or a pageant princess. Her allure wasn't an ethereal aloofness with cheekbones as sharp as glass. On the contrary, her cheeks were round, her plump lips begging to be kissed. Hell, to be fucked.

And she had the long, golden blonde hair of an angel.

She was thin, but still boasted curves, and his fingers longed to follow the shape of her body. Right then, her eyes were cast down as she examined the table, but that didn't matter. He'd memorized the color earlier. Blue, but with a hint of green that flashed like a gemstone in the stage lights. Her eyes were vibrant, as deep and changing as the sea, and oh, how he wanted to dive in.

It had been a long time since he'd truly craved a woman. He loved women, no denying that. And he'd never allow a woman to leave his bed unsatisfied. But most women were mere distractions. Either that or a balm. And when he invited them into his bed, it was always with the knowledge that they'd be leaving. Maybe the next morning, maybe the next month. But it would end. How could it not? There was nothing real between them, after all.

This woman, though…

Something about her intrigued him. Called to him. She seemed both strong and vulnerable at the same time, and when she finally looked up, he saw the flash of an unguarded expression in those sensual eyes. *Longing.* Almost immediately, she shuttered the emotion, a smile finding its way to her lips. She was a contestant, and she'd slipped the pageant mask back on as easily as another woman might slip on a shoe.

But in that brief, unmasked moment, he'd seen a reflection of himself in her eyes. A craving. A need. *A future.*

He had a sudden fantasy of pulling her close. Of kissing her. Tasting her. Of ripping that damn gown off of her so he could see the real woman underneath.

He didn't understand it; he damn sure wasn't going to let himself analyze it. And before he could talk himself out of it, he walked up to where she was eyeing the tiny cheesecakes, as if they were something dangerous that was about to explode.

Without hesitating, he took two and popped them in his mouth, then grinned at her. She said nothing, only stared at him, a polite smile plastered across her face.

For the briefest of instants, his gut did a somersault, which was ridiculous, because he didn't get nervous. Nerves destroyed his edge, and if he lost his edge, he'd lose everything. Hadn't every one of his coaches told him that?

He squared his shoulders, then caught her eye. "I think we're kindred spirits, Miss Fairchild."

"I'm sorry?" She glanced down at the cheesecake, clearly confused.

"Neither of us wants to be here." He nodded his head to indicate the emergency exit, fighting the almost overwhelming urge to grab her hand and whisk her away to a dark room. He longed to touch her. To kiss her. To get lost in the feel of her and the sound of her moans when he thrust his cock deep inside her. He wanted to hear her scream his name and beg for more, and he wanted to hold her close and kiss her tenderly after she'd shattered in his arms.

He took a step back, the craving for her so intense he was certain that she could smell the scent of his desire.

"I-oh." Her eyes were locked on his, and in that moment Damien didn't care if he never moved again.

"Nichole—"

"Nikki." The name came fast and hard. She dipped her head, then licked her lips. "I go by Nikki." She looked back up at him. "Not that."

"Nikki." He felt his lips pull into a smile. "It suits you."

He swallowed, then opened his mouth to speak, though he really wasn't certain what he intended to say. Not that it mattered, as he didn't get the chance to say anything at all. Because that's when Carmela decided to show up, apparently bored with shopping and the suite's amenities.

"Damie, darling." Her accent was thick and as sensual as her pouty lips and mass of dark waves. "Come. We should go, yes?"

He wanted to tell her no, not yes. He wanted to tell Carmela that things had changed. That he was putting her on a plane. That it had been fun, but he knew now what—no, *who*—he wanted.

But he didn't say that. How could he? He knew a few things about Nikki Fairchild. He'd read her contestant's bio. He knew she'd just started college. That she was pursuing a double major. And he knew from her interview that she was ambitious.

She was starting out. He was breaking out.

This wasn't their time. Not yet.

But he'd move heaven and earth to find her in the future. And between now and then, he'd do whatever it took to make sure that he had the means to build that lever.

In the meantime, he'd watch and he'd wait. And maybe, just maybe, he'd be a little less fucked up knowing that a woman like Nikki was out there—and that one day she would be his.

He took Carmela's hand and met Nikki's eyes. "Miss Fairchild," he said with a parting nod.

Then he turned to escort Carmela back to their room, knowing full well that when he had her naked beneath him—when he buried his cock deep inside her—it would be the thought of Nikki Fairchild making him hard.

Chapter Two

Malibu, California
Now...

Damien Stark stood in the doorway of his master bedroom, his gaze fixed on the woman who had teased his mind and stolen his heart all those years ago. The woman he'd craved from the first moment he'd seen her. The woman who was his wife. Who he loved beyond reason.

As far as he was concerned, Nikki was the biggest miracle of his life, the mother of his children, and to this day he didn't know how he'd been so lucky to not only find her, but to keep her.

She was the reason he drew breath in the morning, and she loved him back with equal ferocity, seeing past his faults, his fears, his flaws. Believing in him always.

Even when he failed her.

He closed his eyes, pushing away the darkness that had been edging up on him since the moment his youngest daughter had been taken. A darkness that had been speared with light when they'd gotten her back and he'd once again held Anne tight in his arms.

But that bright moment of hope and relief hadn't changed the single, inescapable fact—*he'd failed.*

He had one job as a father. One job as a husband. To protect his family. And when it had truly counted, he'd completely missed the mark.

His whole life, he'd excelled. Success after success after empire-expanding success. He'd made mistakes, sure. But he'd owned them. Built on them. And none of them had the power to destroy him or the people he loved.

On the contrary, every mistake in his career was a stepping stone to a greater triumph. Another asset to control. Another luxury to acquire. Another industry to master.

And he'd mastered so goddamn much.

But not one iota of that mattered, because the edifice he'd thought he'd built was nothing more than a house of cards balanced on a foundation of smoke and mirrors. And he hadn't even seen the cracks until somebody had pushed into his world and kidnapped his daughter.

A familiar fury raged through him, and he battled it down, just like he'd been doing since the shock of Anne's kidnapping had blindsided him. And just like he continued to do even after getting her back safely one short week ago.

And yet it wasn't the kidnapper who bore the brunt of his rage, though he'd happily squeeze the life out of the son-of-a-bitch with his bare hands. No, Damien's rage was aimed at himself. At his own arrogance. At the lack of imagination that had allowed this to happen, because he'd never seen it coming. They'd had security. They'd had protection.

But it hadn't been enough. Because he hadn't made it enough.

Goddamn shortsighted arrogant motherfucker.

He started to lash out. To pound his fist against the door frame. But he pulled back, not wanting to wake Nikki or the two little angels curled up next to her in their bed. His wife. His precious little girls.

His family.

As much as he loved Nikki, he hadn't truly understood how full his heart could be until he'd held Lara in his arms for the first time. And though he hadn't expected it was possible, his heart had expanded even more when he watched Anne's birth two years ago and saw her draw that first breath.

Every day, his daughters looked up at him with wide, guileless eyes. And every day, he felt that punch in the gut. A fear that he couldn't live up to the trust he saw there. That somehow, someway, he would fail them. Not in the way his own father had failed him. But in some other, fundamental way.

And that's exactly what happened.

He thought of Rory, that fucker who'd taken his child. Of Nikki, broken and huddled in the closet with a blade, blood streaming down her fair skin, cutting for the first time in years. The first time since he'd demanded that she come to him—*to him*—when she needed the blade.

So many times, she'd done exactly that. Gone to him when the burden of the world had been too much to bear. When she needed the pain to find her way back. And he'd always been there for her, his need as potent as hers. Because he had to be the one to take her there. To slide down with her into that sweet place where sensual pleasure crossed over into pain. Where need and desire meshed, merging into euphoria. Where they could both cling to that one small measure of control in a world that was spinning off its axis.

How many times had they saved each other? Their needs meshing as perfectly as their desire?

How many times had he held her close as they fought their demons together?

And yet this time—when the worst parts of hell had swallowed them whole—she hadn't come to him. Instead, she'd put a razor-sharp length of stainless steel against her own flesh, and she'd drawn her own blood for the first time in years.

All because he'd failed her. Because it was his mistakes that spawned the demons.

Because for the first time in their relationship she hadn't trusted him to save her. And why should she, when he'd already failed so spectacularly?

He thought of that. Of the scars on her legs. Of the fresh wound that mocked him still.

He thought—and his stomach twisted with pain and self-loathing.

Mostly, he thought of Anne. His precious girl, who'd been alone and scared for days.

They'd gotten Anne back. They'd talked about Damien's choices. The risks he'd taken to find their daughter and her kidnapper. They'd worked it out, and they were back on keel. And he knew in his gut that Nikki was strong enough to survive the whole ordeal.

But that didn't change the simple, basic truth.

He'd failed.

Roughly, he massaged his palms over his face, then looked again at his girls, curled up together, safe and asleep.

Safe.

For now, at least.

But for the first time in a long time, Damien felt as if the shadows that had plagued his past had returned to haunt him, bringing harsh recriminations and fresh dangers.

He squared his shoulders, steeling himself. He was strong. More than that, he had resources. He had means. And he damn well had the determination to keep those encroaching horrors at bay.

Most of all, he had a life—a family—worth fighting for.

He was fucking Damien Stark.

He'd failed once.

He wouldn't fail again.

Slowly, he drew in a breath, confidence returning. He lifted his phone, intending to check his emails for an update from Ryan Hunter, his security chief, about all the upgrades they were implementing. Instead, he saw the text that only a few moments ago had sent him spiraling back into bittersweet memories of Texas. Sweet, because that night in Dallas was the first time he'd laid eyes on his wife. Bitter, because it had been six long years between that first glimpse and the moment he'd finally held her in his arms.

"Damien?"

He looked up, his body reacting from nothing more than the sensuality of her sleep-heavy voice.

"I'm here, baby."

She pushed a stray lock of blond hair out of her eyes before propping herself up on an elbow. He held his breath, afraid she'd wake the kids, but their two daughters remained motionless. Their oldest, Lara, now four. And their youngest, Anne, whose birthday had been today, Wednesday. Technically yesterday, Damien realized, since it was past one in the morning. Two precious little people, one blond, one dark. Yin and Yang. His girls. His babies. Now sleeping peacefully, worn out from spending the day in the pool with Mommy and Daddy, then snuggling up to watch a Disney movie.

Since their birthdays were so close together, the girls' joint party had been the previous Saturday. And though it had been planned only as a toddler birthday party, the event had become so much more than that. A celebration of life. Of Anne's safe return. And of the capture and incarceration of the fucker who'd had the gall to steal her away.

The only way it could have been better was if Damien had killed the man. Rory Claymore. A spineless excuse for a human who was now behind bars after entering a plea of guilty to two counts of aggravated assault and kidnapping. Now he could rot in prison.

Yesterday had been a smaller, private celebration. Just Damien and his girls, with a homemade chocolate birthday cake for Anne, and a lovely, lazy day celebrating their family.

Nikki blinked sleepily. "Is it morning already?"

"Almost two."

Despite his answer, she glanced at the clock beside the bed. "What are you doing up?"

He allowed himself the ghost of a smile. "I was thinking about Carmela, actually." Now the face of the highly successful designer label she'd launched with her husband, Carmela D'Amato was not only a former fashion model, she was also one of the few women before Nikki that Damien had fucked with any pattern of regularity.

As he'd expected, his wife arched a brow, and that predictable reaction—half-amusement, half-jealousy—raised his spirits considerably.

"Oh, really?" She was awake now, her voice no longer coated with the thickness of sleep. There was, however, a hint of humor, which underscored how far they'd come. Once upon a time, Nikki would have happily strangled Carmela. And considering the games the Italian beauty had played in Germany, Damien would have handed her the rope.

"Care to explain yourself, Mr. Stark? Just because I no longer think of her as the monster bitch queen from hell doesn't mean that I want her filling my husband's head."

"I was remembering Dallas," he said, moving toward her, then sitting on the edge of the bed and taking her outstretched hand. "I was thinking that without her we might never have met."

"Without Carmela?" Her lips twitched. "No way. I give full credit to those tiny cheesecakes."

He chuckled. "The cheesecake was only my excuse to get near to you. The woman who took my breath away the moment I saw her on stage. The woman who still does," he added as he brushed his thumb over her lower lip, satisfaction coursing through him from the way she responded, her eyes closing as she released a soft sigh of pleasure.

"And Carmela fits in how?" The question was soft. Barely a whisper.

"She's the one who urged me to accept the invitation to judge. She wanted to see Texas. Horses and cowboys."

Nikki's delighted laugh warmed his soul. "You never told me that.

And did she find a cowboy?"

"She did. I went back to Milan, then London, then home to LA. She stayed in Dallas. I'm not sure how long they were together. He had a ranch. I think she was particularly fascinated by the longhorns."

"I'll bet she was."

He could tell by the laughter in her voice that she thought he was teasing her, but it was true, though not something he'd thought about in years and years. Everything had changed when he'd walked out of that ballroom with Carmela, and the clever model was savvy enough to pick up on it, and self-assured enough to walk away without throwing a tantrum. She'd left the next night on the arm of a denim-clad, Stetson-wearing millionaire she'd met in the hotel bar.

Carmela had left because of Nikki. And that wasn't the only change she'd wrought unawares. Damien had always held his private life close, but Nikki had gotten under his skin, and after Dallas, he'd accepted even fewer invitations to events and parties. He hadn't shunned women, but as he'd told Nikki early in their relationship, he hadn't dated. He'd fucked. And that only to take the edge off.

There was only her. There'd only ever been her. There would only ever be her.

And what truly made her his miracle was that she felt the same way about him.

"What prompted the trip down memory lane?" She brushed her thumb lightly over his hand, their fingers still twined together. "I like the part about us, but I'm not sure why you felt compelled to work Carmela into the memory. Contrast?" She lifted a brow in question as a small smile played over her lips.

"She sent me a text."

"Oh?" Her eyes dipped to his phone.

"She just heard the news."

"Oh." This time her tone was flat.

"She was embarrassed not to have reached out before. Apparently she and Paolo have been knee deep in prep for their upcoming show. But she's relieved to know that Anne is home now."

"Home." She drew a breath as she shifted on the bed, releasing his hand so that she could touch both of the girls. "Well, I—I mean, tell her we appreciate the thought. I do like her, you know. She's grown on me. Back then—that night in Dallas, I mean—I hated her. I think I hated her at the pageant even more than the night she showed up in your hotel room in Germany."

"In Germany, you were already mine, wholly and completely. In Dallas, there was only the potential."

"Potential, Mr. Stark? Aren't you the one who once told me we were inevitable? That no matter what, we would have found each other?"

"We would have. We're bound, you and I. And somehow, the thread that connects us would have pulled you to me."

Even in the dim light, he could see the storm building in her eyes, a wild passion that filled his soul, both arousing and humbling him.

Christ, she had such power over him, and yet she still submitted. Gave herself to him so openly and willingly.

Trusted him.

He sat back, sighing deeply.

She frowned, then lifted the hand that had been stroking Anne's tiny head and rested it on his thigh. "Come to bed. We can carry the kids back to their room," she added, and he felt his balls tighten merely from the heated suggestion in her voice. "We probably should have moved them already."

"They're fine," he said. "Today was special." They'd spoken with a counselor the day after they'd gotten Anne back, and she'd urged that they keep to a normal routine. That fucking prick Rory had kept Anne drugged, a fact that made Damien's blood boil, but also meant that she now remembered none of it. Or, at least none of it other than the steady stream of Disney movies.

A tiny blessing in a sea of horrors.

As for Lara, she knew her sister had gone away, but her imagination didn't lead her to the nefarious. And now Lara seemed to have forgotten that Anne had even been gone.

"Change their routine too much and it might actually be counterproductive," the counselor had said. And so they'd let the girls fall asleep "accidentally" in their bed that first night. But after that, the girls had returned to their bedroom, a few extra stuffed animals for their comfort—as well as for his and Nikki's.

And although both he and Nikki knew they couldn't work from home forever—and, in fact, were both returning to their respective offices tomorrow—they'd spent the week since Anne's return doing as little work as possible. What they did tackle, they handled from home. The girls, however, were too young to understand the change in routine, especially since he and Nikki both frequently worked from the Malibu house.

Tonight, the whole family had piled into bed for popcorn and *Puppies!*, known to the rest of the world as *101 Dalmatians*. And since the kids had been zonked after a day in the sun—and since it was Anne's birthday and both he and Nikki had wanted the girls with them—they'd let their babies fall asleep in Mommy and Daddy's bed.

"In that case, come to bed with all of us," Nikki urged now. "You can fall asleep holding your wife."

"Soon. I'm going to take care of a few things that have been hanging."

Her eyes scanned his face. "You can't sleep. And it's not just tonight."

He should have known she'd notice. "Just thinking about work." Which was technically true. He needed to shoot some emails to Ryan, and now was as good a time as any to do that. And no, the emails weren't directly related to Stark International's business, but anything relating to the safety and security of the CEO and his family fell under the purview of the Stark International security team, and that was Ryan's purview.

"I can get up. Make you some coffee."

He leaned forward and cupped her cheek, then kissed her sweetly. "It's fine. *I'm* fine. And coffee would only keep me up longer."

"Damien—"

"Go to sleep, baby. And I promise you'll wake up in my arms."

Again, she studied him, then gave him a tight little nod. "I better."

He kissed her again, then slid off the bed. He paused in the doorway and looked back, savoring her sweet smile before she drew the girls tight against her, blew him a kiss, and closed her eyes in surrender to sleep.

Chapter Three

A cup of coffee sat untouched on the dining table in the third floor kitchen as Damien skimmed the email he'd just dictated to Ryan, tapped out a few tweaks, then clicked *send*. He opened a fresh email, intending to draft another note, this one to his brother, Jackson Steele, about the ongoing issues at The Domino, a joint real estate venture between Steele Development and Stark Real Estate.

As a rule, Damien didn't get personally involved with the minutiae of the various projects under the Stark International umbrella. Absent cloning himself, that would be a physical impossibility. He'd been hands-on with The Domino, however. Not only because the impetus had been his own unique vision of what an office complex campus should look like, but also because he intended to eventually move all of Stark Applied Technology—the first Stark entity he'd created back in the day—from Stark Tower in downtown Los Angeles to The Domino in Santa Monica.

As both the architect and co-developer, Jackson had been neck deep in the project from its conception. Recently, he'd fully taken the reins so that Damien and Nikki could recover with Anne after the kidnapping, and Damien had been relieved to have the project watched over by someone he trusted so deeply.

Ironic, considering that for most of his life, Damien hadn't even been aware he had a brother. Half-brother, technically. And when they first met, Damien hadn't trusted Jackson at all. And that distrust had been reciprocated.

But that discord had long ago evaporated. They were family now, as well as friends. And they'd bonded over a shared contempt for their father, Jeremiah Stark. The man who'd kept them apart and had spent their respective childhoods tormenting each in different ways.

He hadn't yet started the email to Jackson when an incoming call notification flashed on his phone's screen. *Ryan.*

He pressed the button to answer. "Trouble?"

"I saw your email. Thought I'd call."

"The morning would have been soon enough."

"I was up anyway. Waiting for Jamie to get home. She's out with Matthew."

"Is she?" A mutual friend, Matthew Holt was fast becoming a legend in town. With shelves full of Grammy Awards, Emmy Awards, and Academy Awards, the producer and owner of Hardline Entertainment had his finger in all aspects of the entertainment industry. He also had a reputation for being reclusive, dangerous, and brilliant. Not to mention being a total manwhore, bedding any woman who showed a hint of interest—single, married, attached, it didn't matter— and then cavalierly moving on to the next.

Of course, Damien knew better than anyone that reputations could be deceiving, but considering Holt's mostly secret ownership of Masque, a private sex club, Damien had reason to believe that the rumors about Holt had some basis in fact. Enough basis that he was surprised to learn that Ryan had consented to let the man escort his wife.

After all, Ryan had a need for control that rivaled his own. More than that, despite the level of kink that Damien knew intrigued both Ryan and Jamie, he also knew that Ryan wasn't the type to share.

"I didn't think that was your style, my friend."

"Funny," Ryan retorted. "Holt tries anything more intimate than guiding her through a room with his hand on her elbow and he'll be making an intimate connection with my fist."

Damien bit back a grin. This was the Ryan he knew well. "So?"

"Holt took her to some Hollywood shindig. Camera crew, the whole nine yards. She's doing interviews with the celebs, then they're going to edit it into a special. It was Evelyn's doing."

"I hadn't heard, but I'm not at all surprised." A Hollywood staple, Evelyn Dodge had represented Damien back in his tennis days. She'd been responsible for keeping his secrets out of the public eye while at the same time making him a fortune in endorsements by being both clever and relentless, not to mention elegant and savvy. She was a woman who said what she meant, never looked back, and had the kind of self-confidence that came from genuine skill and intelligence.

Most of all, she'd always had his back, and he loved her for it. Jamie, he knew, was in damn good hands.

"It happened fast," Ryan continued. "And with the timing—well, I think Jamie figured that Nikki had other things on her mind."

Nikki and Jamie had been as close as sisters since high school in Dallas, and there was rarely a time when one didn't know what the other was up to. Which meant that this was more fallout from the kidnapping.

"The whole thing came together less than forty-eight hours after Anne was home," Ryan said, as if reading Damien's mind. "She'll tell Nikki the next time they're together, I'm sure. Especially since Lacey Dunlop is already seeing red."

Damien didn't purposefully keep up with Hollywood gossip, but he did pay attention to the lives of his friends. And he knew that Jamie had lost her job to the rising entertainment reporter. Who, he assumed, Jamie was now hoping to take down a peg or two.

"Good for Jamie," he said, meaning it. "Nikki's going to be thrilled. Any update on who trashed her office?"

"Nothing firm. My gut says he had nothing to do with the kidnapping. But I wouldn't be surprised if the vandalism turned out to be Breckenridge's handiwork."

"Agreed," Damien said, his temper rising as he recalled the horrible words that had been spray painted on the wall of his wife's then-unoccupied new office space. He hadn't been able to prevent it. And he didn't know for certain who was behind it.

All he'd been able to do was comfort her after the fact, something she repeatedly told him was enough. But as far as Damien was concerned, it barely scratched the surface.

He wanted retribution, but how could he get that without proof?

He agreed with Ryan's assessment that Richard Breckenridge was a likely suspect. After all, the former investor in The Domino had been none too pleased when Damien had cut him loose after a series of #metoo allegations went public.

Damien had originally been thrilled when Breckenridge, the brains behind a high-profile med tech company, wanted a stake. But the scandal had been both vile and credible, and after Damien terminated the relationship, the man had promised trouble. He'd even gone so far as to phone Nikki the day that the vandalism of her office had been discovered. He'd called her a whore for taking a million dollars from Damien in exchange for her portrait and essentially called Damien a hypocrite for cutting Breckenridge out because of the press coverage of Breckenridge's extremely inappropriate advances and non-consensual demands.

Nikki had told him about the phone call the day of the Stark Children's Foundation brunch, and Damien had fully intended to confront the bastard in person the next day, making it very clear that Breckenridge needed to stay far, far away from Nikki.

But that was the morning that Anne had been taken, and suddenly Breckenridge's bullshit phone call had seemed like nothing more annoying than a telemarketer by comparison.

"Any update on the video?" Damien asked, referring to security footage that caught the image of someone who looked like a teen entering the building and carrying a shopping bag that might well have been weighted down with spray paint cans. Someone thin and hooded who just might have been hired to go in and tag the walls.

"So far, still no ID," Ryan told him. "But we may have found some footage of our suspect from another angle. I'll know more soon."

"Good. Keep me posted. Whoever did that to her office is going to pay. And if it turns out to be Breckenridge, all the better." He rubbed his temples, the need to lash out growing in him once again. A need that he'd been battling down more and more ever since Anne was taken. A desire to batter his fists against all the wrongs in the world, and then the growing need for self-flagellation because no matter how much he wished it, that just wasn't possible.

"What else?" he demanded. "Tell me something good."

"I think Quince is taking our offer seriously," Ryan said. "I don't have a sense of what he'll decide, but I think he's giving it due consideration."

"Is he?" Damien was surprised. Quincy Radcliffe was a talented British MI6 agent who moonlighted—apparently with his government's knowledge and unofficial support—for a vigilante organization known as Deliverance. An organization that had been created by billionaire playboy Dallas Sykes for the purpose of tracking down the bastard who'd kidnapped him and his sister when they were teens. It had, of course, expanded into a whole lot more.

Quincy had been an asset to Anne's recovery, and Damien had told Ryan to float the possibility of Quincy becoming a permanent member of Stark International's security team. Considering his role in Deliverance, however, Damien didn't expect Quincy to give the offer any real consideration.

"Deliverance is slowing down," Ryan explained. "I think it's had some difficulty operating. I don't think the government *officially* knows Deliverance exists, but—"

"I get it. The main asset of Deliverance was its ability to fly under the radar. If it's lost that advantage…"

"Exactly," Ryan said.

"I'll speak to Quince myself. If he's on the fence, I want to push him over. And I'm told I can be very persuasive. Or at least my checkbook can."

Ryan chuckled. "You have your moments."

"And the security upgrades?"

"We're finishing the install of the additional perimeter cameras around the Malibu property in the morning. Nikki's office is already complete, and we're upping the garage security at Stark Tower. That'll be complete by end of the day on Monday. But, Damien—"

"I know." His words were sharp. He knew what his friend was going to say. That security around all the properties was already tight. State of the art. And this tweak was overkill. That Anne's kidnapping had been one of those freak things. Maybe a personal, full-time bodyguard could have prevented it, but maybe not.

He knew that. Knew all of that. And it didn't help.

On the other end of the line, Ryan drew a breath. "Damien…"

"I saw an editorial online last night. Some columnist saying I should have GPS tagged my kids. Just a little implant at the back of the neck. No big deal at all. *Idiot*."

"An implant? Fuck that. Theoretically feasible, but you'd need a power source, dedicated satellites, all sorts of shit. Even if you wanted to do it, it's still sci-fi, and you and I both know it."

"I do know it." Ryan was right, of course. The man knew his stuff, after all. They'd met when Ryan had been investigating the possibility of taking his small but prestigious international security company public. Damien had caught wind of the company, investigated it, and had been impressed enough to seek out a personal meeting with Ryan.

He'd ended up buying Ryan out and setting up Ryan's company as a Stark subsidiary. Ryan ran it for a few years, but as their friendship grew, so did Ryan's placement in the overall Stark universe. Now he ran security for all of Stark International.

The man knew the world of security as well as Damien knew the world of tech. And they both knew that human GPS tracking wasn't yet a viable option. Sure, it was technologically feasible, but current research suggested that unlike passive RFID implants that stored information such as name, birthdate, and social security numbers, GPS chips were active. They sent out a constant pulse and required power. And there was some evidence that they could generate cancerous growths. More than that, if the parents could track a child, then so could a kidnapper. Or the government. Or anybody else. All the fucking time.

And God knew the ethical considerations were manifold.

Even so, both his girls did have small trackers that dangled from their personal backpacks or could be attached to shoelaces. The devices were practical, after all, making it easier for parents to locate a child who got lost in a grocery store or mall. Or, in their case, got out of the house and started to wander the massive property.

Nikki's company, Fairchild & Partners Development, was in the final stages of developing a similar tracker that would work in conjunction with their new Mommy's Helper app. That system would have some impressive additional features. As soon as he saw the prototypes, Damien intended to present Nikki and her partner, Abby, with a formal proposal for a joint venture between the Stark and Fairchild companies that would give Fairchild Development enough capital to launch the kind of international campaign the product deserved. And, of course, they'd switch brands, so that it would be Mommy's Helper trackers hanging from their girls' backpacks.

The morning that Anne and her nanny Bree had been taken, however, Anne didn't have her backpack. And even if she had, the devices weren't designed to prevent or foil a kidnapping, and Rory would have undoubtedly dumped it in the parking lot along with Bree's purse.

"Quit beating yourself up," Ryan said gently. "You might be a kick-ass son-of-a-bitch, but you don't control the universe. No matter how much you might wish you did."

"I don't want to. But I don't think it's too much to ask to control my little corner of it."

He couldn't, though. And that simple truth had been haunting him since Anne's kidnapping. Was haunting him still, long after he'd hung up with Ryan.

He felt out of control. Ungrounded. And though he returned to the master bedroom intending to slide under the covers and draw his wife to him, he couldn't make himself walk through the door. He just stood there, watching her moonlit form beneath the sheet and listening to the soft snoring of his two little girls and the purring of their cat, Sunshine, who'd settled in as well.

How could he get into that bed? How could he wallow in their love and trust knowing that he hadn't earned it?

He couldn't.

And as that wild, hard tension welled up again, he did the only thing he could do.

He turned, and he walked away.

Chapter Four

He didn't bother to turn on the flood lights. It wasn't necessary. The huge moon cast the tennis court in an eerie light, enhanced by the reflection off the nearby Pacific.

He moved in the shadows, shirtless and barefoot, wearing only thin athletic shorts, his arms and thighs aching as he moved across the court, returning the torrent of balls as fast as the machine could shoot them over the net.

He'd been at it for an hour, trying to pound himself into exhaustion. Trying to empty his head of the recrimination, the guilt. The feeling of being absolutely powerless despite the whole world believing he held all the cards.

He kept pushing and pushing. Taking his body to the limit. Trying to find the way over. Around. Under. He didn't fucking care, he just needed to get past it. But he never made it. Never hit that wall. Because no matter how hard he pushed, it was never enough.

His muscles screamed. His feet burned. His back ached. But he couldn't stop. It was still inside him, and no matter how much he chased it across the goddamn court, he'd never run it down.

Because he'd lost it. Lost *her*. His own daughter.

"*Fuck.*" His shoulder screamed in protest as he hurled his racquet with all his strength, sending it sailing over the backboard and out into the landscaped yard. "Fuck." That time the word was a whisper, and he followed the sound of it down onto his knees, his hands on the cool acrylic surface of the hard court, then his forehead, as if he was praying for absolution, bowing down to a god or a universe that had turned its back on him.

"Damien."

Her soft voice touched him like an angel's kiss, sending sweet shivers up his spine. He lifted his head, looking up at her. The moon was at her back, illuminating her hair, making her glow. His lips parted. He wanted to tell her she was beautiful. That she was everything.

That he was sorry.

But the words wouldn't come.

She took a step toward him, then stopped, her expression intense. Strained. She carried a baby monitor in one hand, and through the small speaker, he could hear the soft, rhythmic breathing of his children.

He watched, entranced, as she bent over, putting the monitor on the ground. She wore a pink silk robe tied loosely at the waist. She tugged at the sash, loosening the bow, and the robe fell open, revealing the knee-length nightgown she wore when the kids joined them in bed.

She took one more step toward him, and he drew in a sharp breath, realizing that he'd forgotten to breathe.

She lifted her hands to her shoulders, shrugged, and the robe slithered off her body, pooling behind her in a pile of silk.

His chest tightened, and he became suddenly aware of his beating heart. "Nikki…"

She said nothing, just shook her head as she hitched up her nightgown, the hem rising to reveal her bare thighs, her naked sex. His blood pounded in his ears, and he realized he was upright now, sitting on his heels, his knees on the hard surface of the court, his cock painfully hard.

When she pulled the gown over her head and tossed it behind her, it took every ounce of strength in his body not to grab her arm, yank her to the ground, and bury himself deep inside her.

But he didn't. He couldn't.

Not like that. Not when he was this raw. This desperate. This goddamn fucking lost.

"Take what you need." Her throat moved as she swallowed, her legs spread, her hand sliding down to stroke her beautiful waxed pussy.

"Do you think I don't understand?" Her voice broke as she spoke. "Do you think I don't see you? Do you think I don't know? Dammit, Damien, take what you need. Take *me*."

He shook his head. "No." His voice was rough, barely more than the rasp of fingernails against sandpaper.

"*No?* Don't you dare tell me no." Her voice was as coarse as his, but not lost. And not pleading. On the contrary, her words were a challenge. A dare. And when she bent over to grab the waistband of his shorts and pull him up to his feet, he knew that her words were a command as well.

"Goddammit, Nikki." Need pounded through him. For her, yes. For sex, absolutely. But it was more than that. So much more, and he knew that if he took that first step toward her—if he touched her—there would be no going back. He was holding on by a thread now, tight and taut. And damned if Nikki wasn't holding the scissors.

"Don't," he said. "Don't push me. Not now. Not tonight."

Her hand was flat on his lower abs as she took a step toward him, an ephemeral, magical creature alive with light. Fragile and beautiful. Too fragile and too beautiful to withstand the rawness he felt tonight. The violence inside him. The wildness that was fighting to come out.

Right now, he was danger personified, a beast inside him raging to break free. To be set loose so that he could burn through the pain, like a wildfire spreading fast and furious, leaving nothing behind but charred ground and smoldering destruction.

And yet the feel of her hand on his skin was driving him crazy. Carving a hole inside him. A hole that only she could fill. He needed it. Her heat. Their fire.

Needed to obliterate it all. And, dammit, he couldn't fight much longer.

"You want me to come to you when I crave a blade? Then I need you to do the same." Tears trailed down her cheeks as she withdrew her hand, then slammed it right back, this time against his chest. "You bastard. You goddamn bastard." She choked on a sob. "*This* is where you come? To the night and the court and a fucking ball machine? You think that's going to help you battle down the mess that's inside you? Do you?" She shoved him again. "*Do you?*"

He said nothing. The words wouldn't come.

"You know what we are to each other. You *know*." As she spoke, she pressed her palm against her belly, then slid it down, her movements slow and measured. She traced the curve of her body, touching herself, her skin flushing, her lips parting as her breath came in little gasps. And then a low, soft moan of pleasure as she slid two fingers deep into her cunt. She rocked her hips, her soft noises making him crazy. And when she lifted those same fingers to her mouth and sucked, he almost lost his resolve.

But he didn't.

"I can't." He could barely croak out the words. His throat was parched. His mouth like a desert. "Not like this. It's too much. Don't push me, Nikki." He'd die if he truly hurt her, and tonight, he didn't see how he could do anything but hurt her.

"Fuck you, Damien. *Fuck. You.*" The curse was soft, but raw and heartfelt. "You think the world is slipping away? That you've lost control?" She thudded her sex-slick hand against his chest, but this time he caught her wrist, holding her in place.

"*Stop*," he ordered.

She looked into his eyes, naked and defiant. "Make me."

"Nikki." His voice was low. Dangerous. And he saw the heat flare in her eyes.

"You lost control, Damien? The world not behaving the way you want it to? Your wife not doing exactly what you say? You want the control back, Mr. Stark? Then you fucking *take* it back. You can't control the world? So what? Control *me*. That's what we do, Damien. That's what we are to each other."

She blinked, and fat tears streamed down her cheeks. "Goddamn you, Damien. You know what you need. Hell, you know what *I* need. Don't you dare treat me like some fragile fucking thing who's useless to you."

"Goddammit, Nikki," he growled, something hard and tight snapping inside him. He still held her by the wrist, and she stood there, breathing hard, her lips parted, her eyes on fire. She looked alive and aroused and wild. And she was *his*. A goddamn miracle, but he knew it was true. *She was his.*

Fuck it.

He yanked her close, both her wrists held tight in his large hand. He thrust his other hand between her legs, fingers jamming roughly inside her. She arched back with a strangled cry of *yes*, and the last of his hesitation burned away. She knew what she was offering. What she was freely giving. And though it scared him how much he needed it, he couldn't push her away any more than he could be gentle. Because she was right. He had to take what he needed, and what he needed was Nikki. Her body. Her submission.

There would be nothing gentle about tonight. On the contrary, he was going to take and take. Was going to burn through all of it. The pain. The self-recrimination. All gone. All ashes. Until there was nothing left but her. Nothing left but him. Two shells, empty of the pain, and ready to rise like Phoenixes from the ashes, alive and magnificent, and absolved.

She was his salvation. His oasis in a storm of hurt and loss and doubt and failure.

"*Nikki.*" Her name was a plea, a prayer. He bent her back, two fingers deep inside her and his thumb on her clit as he held her in place. He closed his mouth on her breast, biting, tasting, sucking as she writhed, her swollen clit rubbing against his thumb, her body like a live wire in his arms, her heat burning as hot as his own.

"Up," he demanded, though he didn't wait for her to comply. In one motion, he stood, managing somehow to wrap her legs around him. His fingers were free of her pussy, and he held her ass, then stumbled past the doubles sideline until their bodies slammed against the chain link perimeter, the rattle and clang filling the night. "Arms out," he ordered, his voice hard and raspy. "Legs apart. Hold on, baby." He closed her fingers in the diamond-shaped links of the fence. "And don't let go."

She started to speak, but he silenced her with a kiss, wild and frenzied and tasting of blood. He craved her. Wanted to consume her. Needed to hear her cries fill his head and the night. Needed to bury himself inside her and know—truly *know*—that she belonged to him, forever, for always, no matter what.

Now he claimed her breast, tasting her sweetness, reveling in the fact that she was his. That she'd given herself to him so wildly. So willingly.

"Tell me you like this."

"Yes. God, yes."

"Tell me you want more."

"I do. Damien, please. Please, I want more. I want everything."

Her words were like music. An aphrodisiac. A promise and a prayer.

"Tell me how, baby. Tell me what you need." He tilted his head back so that he could see her face, her eyes on fire, her lips swollen.

"You know," she said, and her words shot through him with all their unspoken truth. *He knew*. He knew because she belonged to him.

Because he knew her as well as he knew himself. And he would always, *always*, give her what she needed.

He slid his hand down, then thrust his fingers inside her so that she was grinding against him, fucking his hand. "Is this what you want, baby? Rough? Wild? Do you want me to fuck you hard? To claim you. To make you mine?"

"Damien, *please*." The need in her voice was like a living thing, making him harder than he could ever remember being. He longed to pound his cock inside her, slamming her harder and harder against the fence, making the chain link rattle.

But not yet. Not until they were both on the edge.

"Tell me why," he demanded, his fingers slick with her.

"Because you need it. Because *I* need it. Something to center me. Something dangerous I can hold on to. And I know you'll take me as far as I can go, but never too far."

His heart swelled. "I will always give you what you need."

"*You're* what I need. Please, Damien." The desperation in her voice was palpable, and he couldn't take it anymore. In one motion, he lifted her, tugging her free of the fence as she wrapped her legs around him. He stumbled a few yards down the fence, then laid her out on the chaise that was set up on the court's perimeter.

For a moment he simply looked at her. The rise and fall of her breasts. Her nipples as tight as pebbles. Her pale skin glowing under the moon. So beautiful. And all his.

"Over," he demanded. "On your knees, your forehead down. I want your ass, baby."

She whimpered, then complied. And, dammit, he couldn't hold back any longer.

He took her from behind, his cock sinking deep inside her slick heat, filling her. She cried out, arching back, silently urging him to go deeper, thrust harder.

"Touch yourself," he ordered, twining the fingers of one hand in her silky hair as he used his other hand to tease her ass and make her writhe even more, her moans and soft cries of pleasure making him that much harder.

"Faster," she begged. "Please. Harder."

Her words fueled him, and he fucked her hard and deep, taking what they both so desperately needed, claiming her as he did, because she was his, goddammit. *His.* No matter how much he fucked up, no matter how far off the path he strayed, she would always be his. Always be his beacon back home again. Back to her.

And with that thought, he cried out, his body shattering in time with her own screams of ecstasy. The storm raged through them, and when it passed, he collapsed onto the chaise, pulling her body against his and holding her close. "Christ, baby, did I hurt you?"

"Yes," she whispered. "But not any more than I wanted."

He chuckled, and kissed her shoulder, then realized that she was crying in his arms. Alarmed, he sat up. "Nikki? Baby, what is it? Are you okay?"

He hooked a finger under her chin, forcing her to look at him. "Are you okay?" he repeated, not breathing until he saw her nod.

"Okay? God, Damien, yes. I'm perfect." A laugh bubbled out. "Now I am."

He frowned, but she just smiled broadly.

"Don't you get it?" she asked. "Oh, Damien. Don't you see? I thought I'd lost you. I really and truly thought I'd lost you."

Chapter Five

"Lost me?" They lay together on the chaise facing each other, and he held her close in defense against the chill from the ocean breeze. "What are you talking about?"

She kissed his chin, then tilted her head so that she was looking into his eyes. "Do you remember the girls' party? When it was wrapping up? How we made love in the library?"

"Are you kidding? Of course I remember." She'd amazed him that day. She'd shown him a video that Jamie had helped her make. A video that had since been released to the press, and which had drawn uniformly positive comments and a flood of support.

In the video, she talked about being a cutter. About how she hoped that sharing her struggle would help others, especially teens who were battling self-harm.

More than that, she talked about him. About how Damien had been her rock through the years. How he still was even though she'd gone over the edge and cut during the kidnapping. About how he'd pulled her back. Anchored her.

And about how she knew that he would always be there for her, and how that knowledge gave her strength.

Her words had lifted him up, and he'd pulled her to him. They'd made love on the mezzanine, hidden from view from the last of the party guests.

"You held me as if I was fragile that night," she told him now.

He swallowed. "So now tenderness is verboten?"

"Don't play games with me," she said, her voice firm, but her tone gentle. "Anyone else, but not me. You've spent the entirety of our marriage—of our relationship—telling me I'm not fragile. Which means that when you start treating me like I'm made of glass, I know something's wrong. Damien," she added, her voice breaking, "that's the only time we've made love since we got Anne back."

He closed his eyes, shocked by the realization that she was right.

"Talk to me," she demanded. "Tell me what's wrong."

He wanted to. God help him, he wanted to spill out the words. But how could he confess so much weakness when she needed him to be strong? "I'm fine now," he said, tracing the outline of her body with his fingertip. "Really. I was lost in the dark, but you guided me back." He met her eyes, then kissed her gently. "Don't you know that you'll always be my path back into the light?"

She blinked, tears pooling in her eyes, then leaned forward to rest her forehead on his. "Damien." His name was barely a breath, but it ricocheted through him, full of love and longing. He closed his eyes, his heart pounding. She'd told the world that he was her anchor? The hell with that. She was his—and she always would be.

"Damien," she said again, and this time when she pulled back, he heard the core of steel in her voice. He opened his eyes, and saw that the tears were gone, replaced by a firm determination. For a moment, she studied his face. Then she slid off the chaise lounge and stood as he sat up, surprised.

"I will always guide you back," she said, moving the short distance to pick up the robe, then wrapping herself in it. "And you'll do the same for me."

She picked up his shorts and her nightgown, then brought them to the chaise and dropped them on the cushion beside him while she remained standing. "That's what we are to each other."

"We are," he agreed.

She sat. "Which is why if you won't tell me what's wrong, I will."

He said nothing, but his heart skipped a beat.

"You think you failed." She opened the robe and trailed her finger over the still-raw wound on her thigh. "You look at what I did and you see failure, and no video is going to change that. Do you think I don't know you well enough to understand that?"

He stayed silent, barely breathing, but her words hung like hope in the moonlit sky. And he listened.

"You think you failed, but you didn't. And maybe if it had just been me, you would have seen that. But the universe has been a bitch, and the world that you see is skewed."

She took his hand into hers. "We can't ever erase what happened. And I would give anything—anything—to have spared Anne, you, all of us. But it wasn't your fault." She cupped his cheek and held his gaze. "It was not your fault," she repeated, her voice as soft as a lullaby.

"It was horrible and terrifying and awful, and when she was gone I didn't know if I could survive. But I did, Damien. *We* did. And Anne is okay. Were you even with us today? We played in the pool. We sang stupid songs and cooked burgers on the grill and made a birthday cake. And she wore her yellow floaties and she smiled and laughed and splashed water on her daddy."

She was crying again, tears glistening like diamonds. "Weren't you there with us? Didn't you see the joy today?"

"You know I did." His voice sounded hollow, as if it came from a long way away.

"Then let yourself *feel* it, too," she said. "Because today didn't feel like failure to me. Today felt like love."

He wanted to speak, but the words stuck in his throat.

"Please, Damien. I'm not discounting what happened to our baby girl, but it wasn't your fault." She lifted a hand to his lips when he opened his mouth to protest. "*No.* You didn't fail. Don't you see that? You can't control the world, Damien. But you did what you could. And sweetheart, what you did was wonderful."

She clutched his hands so tightly it felt as though she would crush his bones. "You're the one who realized it was Rory. Who led the way back to him." Her voice hitched with emotion. "And now that asshole is in jail. Because of you, Damien. He's behind bars because *you* made it happen. That's not failure. That's wonderful."

He closed his eyes, her hands held tight in his. He wanted to weep. And finally—*finally*—he let himself surrender to the knowledge that she loved him. And he let himself glory in the knowledge that she trusted him. That she saw beyond his flaws.

The thought made him smile.

"I like seeing that," she said. "Tell me what you're thinking."

"Just that I love you."

She laughed, and the sound filled him with joy. "You mean that I'm right."

He sighed, reveling in the warm rush that came with the return of his equilibrium. He hated what had happened. Hated how powerless he'd felt. Hated that he hadn't been able to reach out his hand and fix everything that was broken in his world. More than that, he knew he would continue hating it.

But maybe it didn't all mean that he was a failure.

More important, he knew that Nikki didn't believe him to be one.

"Yes," he told his wife. "You're right."

"That means a lot," she teased. "Especially from the great Damien Stark."

"Careful, Ms. Fairchild," he countered, shifting on the chaise so he could tumble her down onto her back. He bent over her, kissing her softly. "It's late. Shall we go back in and see if there's room in our bed to sleep?"

"Yes, but not yet." She took his hand and pressed it over her heart. "I know we're together here. But I need to feel it here, too," she insisted, now taking his hand and sliding it between her legs, making his entire body thrum with renewed need.

"Christ, Nikki."

"Make love to me gently this time, Mr. Stark. Never stop making love to me."

He looked at her, bathed in moonlight. He wanted to exalt her to the heavens. To paint her portrait in the stars. But he didn't know how. So he did the only thing he could do. He kissed her and touched her and buried himself deep inside her. And when she cried his name and begged him to never, ever stop, all he could think was that maybe—just maybe—she'd beaten back the demons that had plagued him.

Chapter Six

Damien frowned as he paced the length of the mezzanine. Part of the Malibu home's second floor, the mezzanine overlooked the entrance and the floating staircase that led up to the third floor. Unlike the public area of the second floor, this portion was accessible only by a private elevator or a hidden staircase. It was Damien's refuge. His library and home office. It was where he kept the glass cases that held his memories. Cherished first editions. The awards and accolades that truly mattered to him. Photos of Nikki and the children.

He used the area for work, yes, but that didn't change the fact that he considered it a sanctuary.

Today, Richard Breckenridge had wormed his way into the peace.

Once again, he looked at his computer monitor and the itinerary that Rachel, his executive assistant, had finalized for him that morning. As he'd requested, she'd kept it light. While home with Nikki and the kids, he was handling only the bare minimum. But there were things that needed his attention. And as unpleasant as the reality might be, Breckenridge was definitely on that list.

Fuck.

"Daddy! Breakfast! Can you hear me, Daddy? I don't think he heard me, Mommy."

He bit back a smile, his mood suddenly lighter. He'd already decided that Lara would have a fine career as an opera singer, because the girl definitely had a solid pair of lungs.

"I think he heard you just fine." Nikki's gentle voice was as soothing as a caress, and though he still had a stack of items marked *Urgent* to review, he pushed away from the desk and hurried to the staircase that led from the mezzanine to the kitchen.

"Dadeeeeee!" Anne's shrill cry joined the fray. "Beck-fast!"

"Did someone call me?" he asked as he entered the kitchen seconds later.

"*Baba!*" Lara threw herself into his arms, her use of the Chinese word squeezing his heart. They'd adopted her at twenty months, and though she'd called him both *Baba* and Daddy for a long time after that, more recently she'd taken to only calling him Daddy. Nostalgia washed over him, and he lifted her into his arms, his eyes on Nikki, who stood in front of the griddle with a spatula in her hand.

"Uh-oh," he said to Lara. "Mommy's making breakfast."

"Just for that, you get cereal, Mister."

"Phew," he teased, putting Lara down as Anne squealed, "Pipcakes! Choca pip-cakes!"

"Not today, kiddo," Nikki said. "Scrambled eggs."

"*Mommy!*" Both girls managed the cry in unison.

"Eggs today, pancakes tomorrow," Damien told them. "Whine today, no pancakes tomorrow. Okay?"

He looked at each girl in turn, and though they pouted, they both nodded. "If only all my problems could be handled with such high-level negotiations," he said, making Nikki laugh. "And by the way, good morning."

"Good morning to you, too," she said as he moved to the table and settled in next to Anne. "But what's the matter?" she asked.

"Nothing. Just work."

She tilted her head, her brows raised. "Remember me? I'm the woman who knows you better than anyone."

"You do," he agreed, amused.

She poured the bowl of eggs onto the griddle, then pointed the spatula at him. "We said no more secrets, Damien."

"And I'm not keeping one." He took Anne's sippy cup and refilled it with apple juice. "I'll tell you. I just don't want to poison the morning."

For a moment, she said nothing. "Fair enough. But we're home, and we're safe, and we can handle anything."

Slowly, he nodded. And as she turned back to the eggs, he stood up again, then moved behind her, sliding his arms around her waist and pulling her close.

"Careful, Mr. Stark. Wouldn't want to burn the eggs. Or give the kids a show."

He laughed, and the feel of it in his chest underscored what he already knew—that she was right. They were together. And they would be fine.

"Breckenridge wants to meet with us. And with Jackson. Says he wants to apologize to you. Then he wants to talk to Jackson and me. He contacted the legal department to request the appointment. I haven't responded."

"Oh." She'd gone stiff in his arms.

"That was pretty much my reaction," Damien admitted. "What do you want to do?"

She set the spatula down and put her hands on his, making him hold her even tighter. "I'm not interested in seeing or talking to him. If it's important to him that he apologizes, he can say the words to you. *If you meet with him,*" she added, looking over her shoulder at him.

"Should I?"

He saw the hint of humor flash in her eyes and was relieved. "Asking my advice about the running of your empire, Mr. Stark?"

"Always."

"Liar. But it's a nice thought. Whatever you decide is okay. He was horrible when he called me, but he didn't say anything that hadn't been said before. I did take a million dollars in exchange for posing for a nude painting. And you've talked openly about the way Richter abused you and what happened with Sofia," she added, referring to his former asshole of a tennis coach, who was also Sofia's father. "Hell, you launched a whole charity because of it, and you've helped a lot of kids."

"All true," he said. "But he doesn't get to call you out of the blue and use our pasts as a weapon."

"No," she agreed. "He doesn't."

For a moment they were silent, and he was certain they were both remembering what Breckenridge had said to her that day. She'd told him in detail, and with every foul word, Damien's blood had boiled.

"The incredible Damien Stark and the coach's daughter? So what if he told the world? It still reeks. And he thinks he's better than me? Do you think I don't know what he paid you to do? That painting. That money?

He paid you like a whore, little girl, and then he married you to make you both feel better about it."

Yeah, those weren't words you came back from.

He waited until she'd finished the eggs and had served the girls. Then he took her hand, told Lara to keep an eye on her sister, and led Nikki out of the kitchen.

The third floor was built with entertaining in mind. Ironic, since before Nikki entered his life, Damien rarely entertained. And he'd designed this house before he'd had any hope of finally having his pageant beauty in his bed, much less as his wife.

But serendipity worked that way sometimes, and now this floor was the heart of the house. The open area at the top of the stairs served as a combination living and entertaining area. The kitchen—originally intended to be a small work-kitchen for caterers—was their regular dining spot. The master bedroom was on this floor. And although they'd originally intended for the girls to have rooms on the first or second floors, that had changed after too many trips up and down. Now their daughters shared a room behind the master. And the third floor was the most childproofed floor in the history of architecture.

It was, Damien thought, an exquisite area, even better than he'd originally imagined since now it had love and laughter and life to fill it. And a cat, he added, noticing the way Sunshine sprawled in front of the glass doors that led to the balcony overlooking the Pacific.

But none of that was what he'd brought Nikki into the room to show her.

"Here," he said, standing at the top of the stairs and facing the stone wall and the fireplace. And there, hanging over it, was his favorite piece of art in the world. "It's a work of beauty," he said, easing her in front of him and wrapping his arms around her, his chin resting on her head. "Exquisite."

"Well, Blaine's a very good artist."

He chuckled. "He is. And for this piece, he had an exceptional model."

The painting was a nude, a stunning portrait with erotic overtones. Nikki stood with her face turned away, gossamer drapes caressing her body and her hands bound behind her back with a red sash. Binding her to him, he'd thought, unaware at the time the painting was commissioned just how prescient that image would be.

"He wanted me to be ashamed," Nikki whispered.

"Did it work?"

She shook her head. "I'm proud of this painting. And I'm proud of the money I earned and how I used it to start my own business. But even if you hadn't paid me a dime, I wouldn't have regretted posing." She turned in his arms. "This painting bound us. As tightly as that red cord."

He closed his eyes and bent his forehead to hers, knowing that he shouldn't be amazed that she was voicing his thoughts. "You're everything to me. You know that, right? You and the girls are my life. My breath."

"And you're mine, Mr. Stark. Forever and beyond."

Chapter Seven

"What's the verdict?" she asked later as they were sitting by the pool watching the girls play in the shallow end.

"Verdict?"

"About Breckenridge. Are you going to meet with him? I mean, I think he's swine, but if you think he deserves the chance to apologize, I won't disagree. It's not my decision to make."

"I told Rachel to schedule a meeting tomorrow afternoon. But not because I want to give him the chance to apologize. I want to look into his eyes and get a read on him, knowing what I know now."

She cocked her head, studying him. "You think he might be behind the vandalism at my office."

"I think he's a vile human, and I wouldn't put that kind of thing past him."

She nodded, obviously agreeing.

"Mommy!" Lara's voice cut through the lingering silence. "Can we go down to the playscape?"

Nikki stood, then reached a hand down for Damien. "Come with us? Or are you going to go in to the office today?"

"Trying to get rid of me?" He'd told her he'd probably go back to work this week, and it was already Thursday.

"Hardly." She tossed him a smile as she wrapped Anne in a towel and then reached for Lara. "I love being here with you. But I think your empire might need your attention."

"It has my attention," he told her. "Why do you think I take such care to hire only the most talented people to run every arm of my Stark International in every corner of this planet? They stand proxy to me every day, baby, and I trust them to do their jobs as much as I trust my ability to hire good people." He flashed a quick grin. "I think that trust will hold out for one more day."

"You make a good point, Mr. Stark."

"And what about your empire?" he teased. "Doesn't it need your attention?"

"Manifest destiny may not have pushed my company across the globe yet, but what you just said still applies. Abby's got it under control."

There was a tease in her voice, but he saw the hint of a frown. "I'm sure she does," he said gently as he twined his fingers with hers. "And the girls will be fine when you go back to work. But if you want to work from the bungalow again, you know that you can do that..."

For almost two years she'd used the beachfront bungalow that he'd built for her as a temporary office so that she could be closer to the kids. And, in fact, she hadn't even officially worked from her new office space yet, since the first day of occupancy had fallen in the midst of Anne's kidnapping. Abby, her partner for going on two years, had handled the move-in and the hiring of some new staff. And if Nikki wanted to continue to work remotely, he wouldn't begrudge that decision.

"Baby?" he asked when she remained silent.

She sighed, then smiled up at him. "I don't want that," she said, and he was surprised by how relieved he was by her words. She was strong. He wanted to see her being strong.

"Before, working in the bungalow was my choice," she continued. "I wanted that time with the kids after Anne was born. But then it was my choice to rent the new office and to go back to work away from the house."

Her shoulders rose and fell. "If I go back to the bungalow now, it's like he won. We got Anne back, but Rory will still have won. Does that make sense?"

He cupped her face. "Perfect sense," he said, then kissed her, more relieved than he probably should have been to know that Rory hadn't taken the joy of her work from her as well.

"He changed so many things," Nikki continued, pressing a hand over her heart. "In here. And in here," she added, tapping her temple. "I'll never look at the world the same again. I can't change that, Damien. But I won't give him any more power."

"You're a remarkable woman."

Her smile was thin, but her expression was bright. "I'm very glad you think so."

He laughed, then reached down and scooped up Anne. "I'll tell you what you told me last night, because you were right. We can't heal if we don't move forward."

Her brows rose. "Is that what I said?"

"Not in those words, but it was what you meant. And you were right."

She nodded, then met his eyes. "So we'll both take today, Mr. Stark. Tomorrow we can drive in together."

"I like that plan. Playscape now?"

"We can see the playscape from Bree's patio," she said. "If we're heading back to work tomorrow, it's time to see what she's decided."

Before the kidnapping, their nanny, Brianna Bernstein, had been debating whether or not to move to New York and attend journalism school. Then all hell had broken loose, her boyfriend, Rory Claymore, was revealed as the kidnapper, and even though she'd been taken along with Anne, Bree had stood out like a giant, neon question mark. Was she an innocent girl, used by an evil boy? Or had she been part of the scheme, her own kidnapping nothing more than staged misdirection?

The fact that she was still living on the property and helping with the girls evidenced the answer well enough, but that didn't change the fact that for a while things had been tense, to say the least.

Nikki shot Damien a sideways glance as the kids scampered ahead. "Whatever she decides, it's going to be hard that we didn't trust her. Even under such crazy circumstances."

He nodded. "I know."

In the end, Bree had been instrumental in getting Anne back, but Damien knew that his lack of belief had hurt. And he hated knowing that he'd lacked such faith in someone who loved his children deeply.

He and Nikki had already told her that they would support whatever she decided. She was welcome to stay on as the girls' nanny. They'd help if she wanted to move to New York. And if she decided to walk away from the Starks entirely…

Well, they would regret it, but they would also understand.

With a sigh, he slipped an arm around Nikki's waist. "Those were hard days, and we didn't trust a lot of people we should have. Ollie.

Sofia."

He watched her as he spoke, and he saw the way her face changed at the mention of his childhood friend, Sofia.

"I know she was innocent. And I'm sorry she had a miscarriage. But that doesn't mean I have to trust her." She grimaced. "We have a long history, after all."

He nodded slowly. "You do," he said as he watched their little girls scamper ahead of them. "But my history with her is longer."

A lifetime longer, he thought. He and Sofia had saved each other through an abusive childhood where they'd been thrown together in the worst possible way. They'd clung to each other, and he'd drawn strength from the friendship. But Sofia didn't have his strength. Instead, she got lost in her head. Fixated on Damien. And that fixation had only grown stronger as they'd grown up.

He and Sofia had never had a romantic relationship—not a real one, anyway. But even so, she'd always seen Nikki as a rival. She'd stalked her. Tried to get Nikki to cut. Tried to get her out of Damien's life, all because she thought that if Nikki were gone, then Damien would want Sofia.

He'd been shocked when he learned the truth. When he'd seen Nikki broken and devastated after Sofia's torment.

Most of all, he'd been furious with himself. Because how had he not seen how far she'd gone off the rails? But he'd always had a blind side where Sofia was concerned. She'd been his lifeline back when they'd both been fighting to survive with the horror that her father—his coach—had wreaked on them both.

For years, Sofia had been the talisman keeping him sane. How could he believe the worst of her?

When it came down to a question of her or Nikki, though, there was no choice. Still, he couldn't abandon Sofia entirely. He cut off contact, yes. But he'd financed her treatment. The best mental health and rehabilitation care that money could be. She'd been treated by the most renowned doctors in the world, and she'd been a resident at the best facility he could find. And as the years passed, she'd healed.

She'd emerged with a clean bill of health from her doctors and an ardent desire to make up for the hurt she'd caused people, Nikki included. She'd gone through the twelve steps. She'd made her apologies.

She'd gotten her shit together.

And, yeah, he was proud of her. Despite all the havoc she'd wreaked in his life, how the hell could he not be?

"She's okay now, Nikki," he said softly. "And I know she'll always be a little bit broken, but she's better. She's healing."

"I know she is." Nikki drew a deep breath. "Listen, about that conversation you two had on the beach…"

He tensed. Sofia had always been an albatross in their marriage, and as much as he loved his wife and would always—*always*—side with her when it came down to it, right now he didn't want guilt or recrimination or Sofia between them.

She looked sideways at him, as if expecting him to speak. When he didn't, she shoved her hands into the front pockets of her shorts.

"Nikki?"

"I'm sorry, is all," she said, her words surprising him. "I got all bent out of shape when I found out you were keeping that conversation a secret. But we don't share a brain, Damien, and you don't have to tell me everything. It wasn't fair of me to get angry, especially after you told me that she'd asked you not to say anything."

He sighed, the tightness in his chest loosening a bit. "I don't want there to be secrets between us either, baby. But if someone asks me to keep a confidence, they need to know that they can trust me to do that. Even from you, unless there's a reason to tell you."

"I know. That's what I'm saying."

He nodded slowly, remembering the way the conversation had gone down. Sofia desperate to talk to him. And him agreeing to meet her surreptitiously on the beach. Sofia had told him about her miscarriage. About feeling lost and alone. And she'd begged him not to say anything to Nikki.

He'd sympathized, and since there was no reason to break her confidence, he'd agreed to stay quiet. But he still shouldn't have lied to his wife.

"What do you mean?" Nikki asked when he said as much.

"You asked me about it the next morning. You saw me with a woman on the beach, and you asked who it was. I lied."

"You said it was Jenny."

"I did. That's when I should have told you about Sofia. Not what she said—I was right to keep her confidence—but I should have told you it was Sofia, not a neighbor. And I should have specifically told you that she entrusted me with a secret. Which means I broke the marriage rules. And I'm sorry."

"Thanks for that." Nikki's lips twitched. "Of course, I still would have wanted to know. But," she added on a sigh, "I would have understood why you stayed quiet. At least until Anne—" Her breath hitched. "You know."

"You're right. Once Anne was taken, all bets were off. After that, I couldn't have stayed quiet about Sofia and the miscarriage."

"But before…" She nodded slowly. "Yeah, I get it. And Ollie? You didn't tell me that he'd asked to borrow money, either."

"Yeah, well, Ollie's a prick," he said, making her laugh.

The lawyer-turned-FBI agent might be one of Nikki's best friends, but he was also in love with her. Or he had been, and Damien couldn't actually imagine any man ever getting over Nikki. "Plus, again, he asked me not to."

"Hmmm." Amusement lingered in her voice. "I suppose that's fair." She shot him a sideways glance, then took his hand. "But you do like your secrets, Mr. Stark."

"I've lived with them my whole life. They're like old friends."

She laughed, and the sound filled his soul. "I get that," she said, then tugged him to a halt before rising up on her toes to brush a kiss over his lips. "But introduce your wife to those friends every once in a while, okay?"

Chapter Eight

"I get it," Bree said. "I really do."

They were on the back porch of the guest house—Bree's home while she worked as their nanny. A few yards away, the girls laughed and giggled on the playscape, Anne in the sandbox, and Lara on the horse-shaped swing.

"I'm glad you understand," Nikki said, sipping the coffee Bree had offered as she leaned against Damien on the small wicker love seat. "But we're still so, so sorry."

"It's okay. I know you have to do everything you can to protect those babies." She pushed a lock of long dark hair off her face. A mix of Jewish and Native American, Brianna Bernstein had an exotic beauty in addition to her sweetness and composure. "They're your priority."

"They are," Damien agreed. "And I'm sorry it hurt you—us not trusting you. *Me* not trusting you. But I wouldn't—*couldn't*—do it differently."

"I know. It's just...I love those girls like they're my own. But they're not. And I think … I think in some ways I've been hiding behind this job. Using it as an excuse not to get out into the scary world."

"It doesn't have to be scary," Damien said. "Considering what you went through, I know that's hard to believe, but—"

"My grandfather was a kid when he escaped from Poland during the war," she said, cutting off his words. "His parents died in a gas chamber. Maybe the world doesn't *have* to be scary, but it usually is." She licked her lips, then looked from him to Nikki. "I always felt safe here, though."

"And then I took that away from you," Damien scoffed.

Bree shook her head, her dark eyes wide. "No—Oh, God, no. Rory did that. What he did to you guys—to Anne—was horrible. But *he* hurt me. *He* used me. You didn't take anything from me. You were just protecting your family. I get that. Really, I do."

Damien nodded, appreciating the words even as he wished he could have done things a hell of a lot differently. At the same time, he knew that under the same circumstances, he would have done the very same thing. Because in the end, Bree was right. His priority was his daughter.

Beside him, Bree pulled her feet up onto her wicker chair, then hugged her knees to her chest. "I don't go to Upper Crust anymore."

"Because of Rory?" Nikki asked.

Bree lifted a shoulder. "Stupid, but that was where we had our first date. And I met him through Kari," she added, referring to one of the managers at the popular Malibu bakery that was a favorite weekend spot for Damien and Nikki. "We're still friends, though. And I asked a couple of days ago. About him, I mean. She said that he'd been coming to the bakery for about three months before the kidnapping. But he'd started asking about me after just few days."

"He targeted you," Damien said. "We already assumed as much."

"I guess. Still makes me feel dirty."

"I get that," Nikki said.

Bree rolled her eyes, looking like a lost teen instead of a woman in her twenties. "I can't believe I went all ga-ga over his name. Rory Fucking Claymore. I told you he sounded like a romance hero, remember?"

A ghost of a smile touched Nikki's lips. "I remember." The smile morphed into a grimace. "I probably should have warned you off him right then, what with a last name like that."

Bree frowned. "What are you talking about?"

"Nothing. Just being silly. I hadn't even realized it at the time, but his last name is the same as this creep I used to know."

Creep was putting it mildly. The first time that Nikki had revealed her scars to Damien, she'd been an emotional wreck, and as far as he was concerned, Kurt Claymore shouldered all the blame. Even now, Damien's blood boiled with the memory. He'd wanted to kill Kurt. To look the bastard in the eyes and squeeze the life out of him.

He hadn't—over the years Damien had learned to control his temper—but he'd still managed a sweet bit of payback. And that had felt pretty damn good.

To this day, Damien didn't know if Kurt or Nikki's mother, Elizabeth Fairchild, had hurt Nikki more. He didn't care. They were both vile, and he'd done everything in his power to keep them out of her life and to avoid the specter of their memories.

Which was why he hadn't told her before that he'd noticed the similarity in names. Or that, just to be sure, he'd investigated Rory's family tree to make certain the two men weren't related. They weren't by blood. But they still had the common thread of being total assholes.

Across from them, Bree sighed, sliding her feet back to the wooden porch as she took a long sip of coffee. "At any rate, point being, he sought me out because I work for you guys. He used me to get to you."

"He did," Damien agreed. "And we're sorry."

"I know," Bree said, smiling at them each in turn. "I really do know."

"Have you decided what you want to do?" Nikki asked.

"I think so." Bree twisted her hands. "I'm still nervous, but I'm going to go to school. I love it here, and I love the girls—but I have to figure out what I want to be. *Who* I want to be." She drew a breath, then exhaled noisily. "I was hoping to stay here through the summer—give you guys time to find a replacement—and then head to New York a week or so before school starts so I can find a place to live and play tourist a bit."

"That sounds fine," Nikki said.

"And you don't have to worry about a place," Damien added, as both women turned to him in confusion. "You have an apartment."

"I—what?" Bree looked at Nikki, who just lifted her shoulders, looking a little lost.

"Call it severance," Damien said firmly. "And don't get too excited. It's only a studio. But it has a doorman and it's not far from the school."

"But—"

"I'll put a trust in place to cover taxes and annual assessments. I'll make sure there's enough principal in the trust that it should generate income to cover those costs for at least the next ten years. By that time, you'll be settled and can pay on your own, or you'll have sold the place. Or rented it."

"I—but—I mean, *severance*? That's not usually a gazillion times more than someone's annual salary. I mean, Mr. Stark—"

"Damien."

"Mr. Stark, that's too much."

"No, it's not," Nikki said gently, and Damien released a small sigh of relief. Normally, he would have consulted Nikki, but he'd made the decision to give Bree the small Manhattan studio he'd bought a decade ago on the spur of the moment. Now, he squeezed Nikki's hand, relieved when she squeezed back, her smile as sweet as sunshine.

"He took you." Damien spoke gently to Bree, trying to make her understand that this was important to him. "You were watching our daughter, and he took you, too. Because of who you work for. Who I am. And you didn't once resent me for that. You thought only of our little girl. You watched over her. Comforted her."

"How do you know I did?" Her voice was low, shaky with unshed tears.

"Because I know you, Bree." He'd failed her, too. He'd been so busy trying to protect his family that he'd forgotten that she'd become part of that family. "Take the condo, Bree. Please." He needed her to. It was part thank you. Part apology.

Then he saw the tears flood her eyes and her mouth tighten as if she was fighting off a deluge. She nodded. "Thank you," she whispered. "This really does mean the world."

"It does," Nikki said, lifting his hand and kissing his fingers.

For a moment, they were all quiet, with only the little girls' giggles filling the air. Then Damien's phone chirped, and he jumped. Nikki laughed nervously, and Damien rolled his eyes, unsure why they should all be on edge, as if they didn't deserve a moment of happiness and calm.

Then he glanced at the display, saw that the call was from Charles, and felt the foreboding rush back. He had no call scheduled with Charles-the-attorney today. And Charles-the-friend wouldn't bother him on a day he was staying home with the girls.

"What's going on?" he asked, ignoring the polite preliminaries.

Charles knew him well enough to cut to the chase as well. "Rory's attorney just called. He wants to meet with you and Nikki tomorrow afternoon. Five o'clock. Before he's transferred."

"Transferred?" Damien repeated.

Beside him, Nikki's forehead creased.

Rory, he mouthed.

"He's in the Men's Central Jail downtown. They're moving him to the LA County State Prison in Lancaster."

"He's not withdrawing his plea, is he?"

Both Nikki and Bree stiffened.

"No. No, the plea's been entered. He's being sentenced on Monday. Probably just a capacity thing."

Damien switched the phone to speaker. Nikki had a right to hear this. Bree, too, for that matter. "Then why does he want to see us?"

"I don't know. But I think it's worth finding out."

He met Nikki's eyes. She nodded, her face going pale.

"All right," he said. "I guess we'll go see the son-of-a-bitch."

Chapter Nine

Bree stayed at the playscape to watch the kids while they went back to the house so that Damien could call Ryan and Jackson and give them an update on the Rory situation. They held hands as they followed the path, walking in silence. At least until Nikki tugged him to a stop where the path crested a small hill, opening up to a stunning vista of the property falling away toward the beach with the majesty of the Pacific in the distance.

"It's beautiful," he said, sliding an arm around her waist and gazing out over the view.

But Nikki wasn't looking at the sea. Her eyes were fixed on him, and he turned to her with a frown. "What's wrong?" As far as he was concerned, the talk with Bree couldn't have gone better. "Nikki?"

"What you said to Bree. About this happening because of who you are..."

He turned away, frustrated. "Don't say it's not true. We both know that it is. Anne wouldn't have been taken if it wasn't for me. Rory took her because of who I am. Because she's *my* daughter."

He watched her throat move, but she didn't speak, and he felt the waves crash over him. He'd spoken the truth because he had to make certain that she understood. No matter how much it might hurt, he needed her to face that horrible reality.

But now that she was staring dead at the reality of their life together, it felt like he was drowning. Because how could they be together when everything he'd spent his life working for was a lever that pushed them apart?

An eternity seemed to pass before she said, very plainly and very simply, "I know. Damien, of course I know." She leaned forward and kissed him tenderly. "And I hate that something so admirable in you was a magnet for tragedy and pain. But that doesn't make it your fault. Would you blame a beautiful woman for being raped?"

Revulsion shot through him. "Of course not."

"Then don't blame yourself for what that asshole did to Anne. To us."

He closed his eyes, wanting to battle back her words, but he couldn't. The truth was that her arguments were the ones he would make were the tables turned. "You're a smart woman, Mrs. Stark."

She tilted her head back for his kiss, and he surrendered to the pleasure of his wife sliding into his arms. She tasted like morning dew. Like the ocean, spreading out toward infinity. Like promise and hope and an eternity together.

She tasted like happiness, and once again he wondered what he'd ever done in the whole of his life that had earned him the value of this moment.

Her hands clutched his hips, providing balance as she leaned back and met his eyes. "Do you know what I want right now, Mr. Stark?"

"The same thing I do." A hint of smile tugged at his lips. "To blow off these calls until later and go see the kids."

She laughed with delight. "God, I love you."

"That works out well," he said, bending to claim her mouth. "Because I love you beyond all reason."

* * * *

"Castle, Daddy! Bigger!"

"Bigger, huh?" Damien filled a second bucket with damp sand, packed it in tight, then overturned it on top of the pile of sand that already existed in the box. He removed the plastic bucket, sat back, then watched as the sand crumbled away.

"No, Daddy!"

"Sorry, squirt. I think if you want a castle, Daddy can write a check. And if you want a custom built one, you're going to have to talk to your uncle."

"Unca Jackson here?"

"Not right now. But I'm sure we'll see him soon."

She pondered that, then looked over toward the swing set, where Nikki was pushing Lara higher and higher, to the little girl's squeals of delight.

"Me, too, Daddy!" Anne lifted her arms. "Me swing, too!"

"That I can handle," Damien said, scooping her into his arms and taking her to the toddler swing. He buckled her in, her little legs kicking with excitement. Then he stood behind her and pushed gently as she squealed with glee, so utterly fearless it made his heart ache. And made him remember the terror he'd felt the day she'd been born.

Not because there had been any trouble with her birth. On the contrary, according to Dr. Tyler, once Nikki got past that touch-and-go first trimester, everything was textbook perfect, including the actual birth. Nikki's water had broken. She'd calmly asked Damien to drive her to the hospital. She'd been admitted. And ten hours later they had a daughter with perfect Apgar scores and the sweetest little face that Damien had ever seen.

But until that moment when they'd brought her home—until she was real and solid and crying in her bassinet—it hadn't seemed real. And he'd gone through the entire pregnancy walking on eggshells.

They'd already had Lara, of course, and he couldn't be happier. But he also didn't think that he could shoulder the burden of another miscarriage, and he was certain that Nikki couldn't. They'd lost Ashley— their first unborn child—to a miscarriage that resulted from Nikki's rare uterine condition. And although Dr. Tyler had assured them that the chances of another miscarriage after the first trimester were slim, Damien had held his breath every single day.

By the time he held Anne in his arms, he felt like they'd dodged a bullet.

He'd never felt that way about Lara. On the contrary, they had Lara because they'd fought against a fate that would have left Lara struggling in an orphanage. They'd found her, then fought for her. Nikki had bared her soul to the adoption agency and the home study counselors. She'd sat down for multiple sessions with counselors about her cutting. They'd worked out a plan to address the surgeries that Lara would need because she'd been born with an extra toe on each foot.

They'd fought for their first child, and they'd won.

But Anne had been an accident. They hadn't even been trying to get pregnant. Just the opposite, since they knew that the odds of Nikki carrying to term were so slim. And as much as Fate had given her to them, Fate could rip her away again.

But Damien wouldn't let that happen. He'd die before he let anyone hurt his daughters. At least, that's what he'd told himself. And then Anne was taken, and there'd been nothing he could do. Not a goddamn thing.

"We were lucky," he said, his voice low. Steady.

Beside him, Nikki turned from where she was helping Lara out of her swing. "Lucky?"

"With Anne. With Rory."

Her eyes narrowed as she studied him, obviously trying to read his mind. "Bullshit. We make our own luck, Damien. You've told me so over and over again."

He just shook his head, then unbuckled Anne, who was struggling to get free and follow her sister.

"Don't do this to yourself," Nikki said, stalking toward him as Anne scurried toward Lara. "It wasn't luck. It was *you*. You're the one who found the clues that led us to Rory. You're the one who put together the team. You're the one who set up the tracking particles so we could tie him to the cash."

"The tracker?" He lashed the words out at her. "You mean that same tracker that was the reason you cut?"

"*I* cut, Damien. Me. Because I was lost and I was scared and my daughter had been taken from me." She spoke low so that the kids couldn't hear. But for Damien, there was no missing the ferocity in her words.

"I was wrong not to have told you."

"Hell yeah, you were. And I'm sure you'll do something again that pisses me off. But that doesn't change the fact that you're ninety-eight percent of the reason that we got our daughter back."

Her phone rang before he could respond, and he was grateful.

"Do you need to take it?"

"It's Frank," she said, referring to her father. She slid the phone unanswered into the back pocket of her jeans. "It's fine."

Damien stayed quiet, studying her. For most of her life, Nikki hadn't known her father. And though there'd been some suspicion as to his motives when he'd stepped back into her life recently, he'd proven to be a genuinely good man.

A travel photographer, he'd been away during the kidnapping. And though she'd said nothing, Damien was certain it bothered Nikki that he hadn't rushed home when he'd learned of their tragedy.

"Talk to me," he said gently.

"It's just—"

"Daddy!" Lara called. "Come here, Daddy! Come see!"

"Just a minute, sweetie!"

"It's not important."

"Yes," he said. "I think it is."

Her smile was thin. "Comparatively, it's not. Your daughter needs her daddy now." She tilted her head. "Go on. I'm fine."

He went reluctantly, but his heart ached. Because he was afraid that Nikki needed her father, too. But that somehow she'd lost him all over again.

He tried not to worry as he went to Lara, then followed her around the back of the guest house where they'd seen a bunny a few days before. This time, however, there were no signs of rabbits, and he took the two disappointed little girls back to the playscape, assuring them that the bunnies were probably off somewhere. Maybe in their warren watching *Puppies!*

Lara rolled her eyes. "Bunnies don't watch movies, Daddy."

"Learn something new every day." He kissed his daughter and looked for Nikki, but only found Bree on her patio.

"She said to tell you she went to the bungalow."

"Is she calling Frank?"

Bree just shook her head. "Not sure."

He considered giving her space, but that didn't sit well. And after asking Bree to watch the girls, he headed down the path to the beachfront bungalow he'd built for her after she'd complained that the only flaw of the Malibu house was that it didn't have easy access to the beach.

He found her in their bedroom standing in front of their newest art acquisition. Another Blaine original, in much the style of the portrait the artist had painted of Nikki.

Whereas that one was bright and vibrant, though, this painting had a sadder, more subdued feel. The color scheme was mostly blue, unlike the vibrant reds and sensual blacks and grays that dominated much of Blaine's earlier work. In the painting, the woman was bound to a chair, and though her sex was hidden in shadows, her legs were spread wide, giving the painting a raw, edgy quality rather than a more sensual eroticism.

They'd found the painting in a gallery, and he'd touched her secretly as they looked at it. Teased her. She'd melted in his arms, and he'd bought the painting because he wanted that memory, always.

In deference to the children, it now lived in a shuttered frame, revealed only when the kids weren't in the room.

"It's so melancholy," Nikki said as Damien came up behind her, sliding his hands around her waist much as he'd done that day in the Beverly Hills gallery. "I think he misses her."

"Who?" he asked, assuming that the *her* was the woman in the portrait.

"Evelyn," Nikki said. "Blaine's paintings have become more melancholy. And even though I'm not sure they've officially broken up, I also don't think they're together anymore."

"No," Damien agreed. "I don't either."

"There was a pretty significant age difference between them. Blaine's what? Mid-thirties. And Evelyn's got twenty years on him?"

"About that," Damien agreed.

Nikki nodded, still not turning around. "They were good together, but I never really saw them as long term. Maybe Blaine did, though. Maybe that's why his new paintings are melancholy."

"Perhaps. Or perhaps he's just an artist working on his style. Either way, Evelyn deserves a partner. Someone who's here for her. Blaine's spending most of his time exhibiting in Asia these days."

"I'd fantasized that maybe she'd get together with my dad."

"They might," Damien agreed. "I know they've been spending a lot of time together."

She turned in his arms, pressing her face against his chest. "I called Evelyn. I don't think—I don't think it's going to work out."

He frowned, confused, then took a step back. He used his finger to tilt her chin up so that he could look in her eyes. "What's going on?"

"He called her from Stockholm a few days ago. Long after I left the message telling him what happened. About Anne," she added unnecessarily. "He told her why he hadn't rushed right back."

There was a harsh lilt to her voice, and he stiffened, fearing the worst.

"Why?"

"Because he was scared." The words were full of disgust and disappointment. And heartache, too.

"Oh, baby."

"Scared? *He* was scared? What kind of bullshit is that?" She drew in a breath. "That's what Evelyn told him. I didn't even get the chance. I guess he was too *scared* to call me and own up."

"I'm sorry. I'm so, so sorry." Considering his own father, he'd been leery when Frank turned up. But the kind photographer had won him over. Now, he couldn't help but wonder if it was a goddamn epidemic. God knows he hoped not. Neither Frank nor Jeremiah were the kind of father that Damien wanted to be.

"Evelyn was here for us," Nikki said. "It was hard and it was horrible, but she was here, right in the thick of it. And she's not even my mother. Or yours. But my real dad—a man who actually took the time to seek me out—he just couldn't be bothered because he was *scared*. Like our life is a fucking Disney park and he only wanted to ride the carousel. Not leap onto the Tower of Terror."

He held her by the shoulders, pushing her gently back so that he could see her face. "He screwed up, baby. I won't argue. But it's hard being a parent. And he's pretty new to the job."

"So are you. You haven't screwed up."

He wasn't entirely certain that was true.

"And you would never bolt if one of your kids was in pain," she added.

"No. I wouldn't."

"Yeah, well, he's done it to me twice. First by leaving back when I was little. And now by staying away when I needed him." A single tear trickled down her cheek. "He could have helped, Damien. But he didn't even try."

He sighed, wishing he had the words to make it better for her. "I won't defend him. But I will say that you need to talk to him."

Her eyes flashed. "Why the hell should I?"

"If I screwed up, would you tell Anne and Lara to turn their backs? To not talk to me?"

"You wouldn't do—"

"Wouldn't screw up? I hope you're right, but it's happened once or twice."

That earned him a tiny smile.

"Just talk to him, baby. He's not your mother. He's trying. Or at least he was. Talk to him and find out why he stayed away. Was he uncomfortable? Unsure what to do or what to say? Afraid of making a misstep?"

She wiped her eyes, then studied his face. "You haven't screwed up, you know. You're an incredible father."

He hadn't even realized he was carrying that fear, but her words released it, tossing away the weight of his own doubts as if they were as negligible as cotton fluff.

"You're amazing," he said.

"That's why we're so good together," she said. "Because I think the exact same thing about you."

She turned and leaned against him, and he put his arm around her as they looked at the painting. "I'm glad we bought it," he said. "And not just to memorialize one wicked afternoon in an art gallery."

"You have other wicked memories of this painting?"

He chuckled. "Not this one. But it occurs to me that the first time I kissed you we were surrounded by Blaine originals."

"That's true. You told me you were going to kiss me that night, and then you did. I've always been impressed by a man who keeps his word."

"We were on a velvet bench, hidden in an alcove. And I'd been fantasizing about that kiss ever since I met a woman with a fascination for cheesecake at a pageant in Dallas."

"And it only took six years," she teased. "You don't move very fast, do you, Mr. Stark?"

"Some things are worth waiting for."

"Like that kiss?"

"It was magical," he told her, then bent his head to hers and kissed her softly and sweetly. "It's even better now."

She sighed happily, and he was struck by the reality that she was truly his. Maybe there really was magic in the world.

"What are you thinking?" she asked.

"That people who say that love at first sight is a myth are both foolish and sad. I loved you from the moment I saw you, and though I don't know how it's possible, I love you more each day. You fill me up, Nikki. You make me feel as though I own the world and everything in it."

Her smile bloomed. "Well, you pretty much do."

"Ah, but you are more precious to me than rubies, and nothing I own or desire can compare to you."

"You better be careful," she said, wrapping herself in his embrace. "Otherwise, you're going to end up spending the whole rest of the day between my legs."

"Trust me, Mrs. Stark, I'd have no objections at all."

Chapter Ten

"It's weird going back today."

Nikki's words filtered through the hall to Damien as he moved from the bedroom toward the kitchen. But she wasn't speaking to him. Instead, she was talking with Bree, who was back on nanny duty.

"I guess it would be," he heard Bree reply. "Just take it slow. And it's Friday, so that's a good way to ease in. Take care of what needs to be handled, then take the weekend to regroup. Start fresh next week."

"You're very wise," Nikki said, and Damien heard the tease in her voice.

"It's true," he said as he came into the kitchen, delighting in the squeals of greeting from his two little girls at the table with their nanny. Nikki stood at the counter, and he let his gaze slide over her, reveling in the way her smile brightened the morning. Then he turned his attention to Bree and the girls. "So what do you three have planned for the day?"

"Puppies!" Anne said, making Bree laugh and Lara roll her eyes.

"Not puppies, silly," Lara said. "Puppets."

"We're going to put together the puppet theater," Bree explained, referring to the birthday present from Jamie and Ryan. "And then I thought we'd make some paper-mache puppet heads and use scrap material to make their clothes. My mom and I used to do that."

"Sounds messy," Nikki said. "Try not to paper-mache the entire playroom."

"We'll do our best," Bree said, obviously fighting a smile. "Won't we, girls?"

"Puppies!" Anne said again, to which Lara responded with her hands on her hips and a shake of her head, looking so damn adult that

Damien had to turn away so she wouldn't see him laugh.

"We should go," Nikki said, kissing each girl in turn. "I want to pop into Upper Crust and get some treats for the office."

"Good idea." He grabbed his watch from where he'd left it on the pass-through bar, then cursed as he glanced at the display.

"What is it?"

"Nothing. Just missed a call." He flashed her a heated look. "Probably came in while we were showering. A small price to pay."

"True enough. I missed one, too. Guess we really are diving back into the deep end of the work pool."

He pulled out his phone and frowned at the display, then looked back up at Nikki. "Who called you?"

"I don't know. I didn't recognize the number and there was no voicemail. Why?"

He turned his phone so that she could see the display. "Sofia."

"Oh." She snagged her phone off the charging stand on the counter, then passed it to him. "She's not programmed into mine. Is that her number?"

He glanced down, and Nikki must have read his expression, because she said, "Guess she really wanted to get in touch with us. Did she leave you a message?"

"None," he said. "But she knows I'll recognize the number. Presumably, she's expecting me to call back."

"I guess you can call her back from the car."

He almost laughed at her pageant perfect expression, but he knew better. Whatever detente she and Sofia had reached since Sofia's apology and Lara's adoption, it was a tenuous one.

"It'll be easier to just wait and call her from the office," he said. "You ready to go?"

Her eyes darted to the kids, and for a moment, he thought she was going to shake her head and tell him she'd changed her mind. That she wanted to spend one more day at home and start fresh at the office on Monday.

But then she squared her shoulders, grabbed her leather tote, and nodded firmly. "Absolutely, I am."

After hugs and sloppy kisses, they finally found their way into the elevator and then down to the underground walkway that led from the house to the garage, one of his favorite features of the property.

Nikki called it the Bat Cave, and he supposed she had a point. Damien had always loved cars—their sleek beauty. The power of a well-built engine. As a teen on the tennis circuit, he'd had to limit his fascination to behind the wheel. But once he'd left the sport, he'd had the time to indulge his passion. There'd been little time in the early days, of course. Building an empire was a twenty-four/seven endeavor. But he stole hours here and there, relieving the stress and pressure of the world he was creating by re-creating something of beauty from the past.

Now, years later, he had an impressive collection, both of cars he'd bought outright because they appealed to him, and of cars he'd rebuilt himself, taking deep satisfaction in the meticulous process of restoration. And he kept all of them in a twenty-car underground parking garage camouflaged to look like part of the Malibu hills.

"Boys with their toys."

He glanced at his wife, and she laughed.

"I'm talking about the rapturous expression on your face."

"Well, it's a rapturous room."

She rolled her eyes. "Like I said…"

He pressed a hand against her back, guiding her toward the eighth row and the Rolls Royce Phantom he'd restored a few years ago. "If I recall, you've gotten some enjoyment out of my toys, too."

"All of them," she said, sidling up to him, then kissing him lightly as her hand cupped his balls.

"Careful, Ms. Fairchild."

"Or what, Mr. Stark? You'll make me late for work? I own the company, remember?"

"True enough. My wife is a badass in the business world."

"And don't you forget it."

He watched, amused, as she turned around, scanning the cavernous garage. Then she moved away, following the line of cars slowly, her gaze taking them all in.

"Something on your mind?" he asked.

"This one." She stopped at the driver's side door of his shiny red Bugatti Veyron. The very car he'd driven on their first date. Or, rather, he'd driven it to the airport so that they could fly to Santa Barbara for lunch. And it wasn't so much a date as a step in the negotiations of the terms for her portrait. Either way, he'd been hard from the moment she'd burst into his office, ready to spit fire. But the real heat came later when he held her in his arms and knew that he would never let her go.

"Yes," he said, his voice rough with emotion. "This one is perfect."

"Definitely." Considering the rawness in her voice, he was certain that her thoughts tracked his own, and it took all his willpower not to bend her over the polished rear of the car and fuck her hard and fast, just to claim her once again.

"Damien?"

He saw the flush on her skin, her nipples hard beneath the thin silk top. Her lips were parted, and her chest rose and fell with her breathing.

He met her eyes, his brow rising in question.

"Yes" was all she said, but it was enough. He held out his hand, and she walked to him, slipping out of her heels as she did. She wore no stockings, and was now barefoot on the polished concrete floor that Edward kept pristine.

He turned her in his arms so that his erection was pressed against her back as he slid his hands down over her hips, then along her thighs to the hem of her pencil skirt. He started to ease it up, but she stopped him by cupping her hand over his. "No. Take it off."

He said nothing, but moved his fingers to quickly unfasten the button at the back, then ease down the zipper. Tucking his thumbs under the waistband, he shimmied it down over her hips, leaving her clad below the waist in only a pair of black panties with a lace back.

Slowly, he stroked his hand over the lace, following the curve of her ass. "Do you like that?"

"Yes," she murmured.

"Good. Take them off."

She turned her head to look at him over her shoulder. "Take them off for me."

"With pleasure."

With pleasure. The words seemed to hang in the air as if their shared passion had conjured them.

With Nikki, everything was *with pleasure*, and his entire body burned with the truth of that. Every breath he drew. Every touch of his skin against hers. Every look, every whisper, every touch.

Every atom within him hummed and swirled with only one purpose—Nikki. She was light and love and romance and candles. She was sex and sin and pain and longing.

She was his, goddammit, and in that moment he was pretty damn sure he'd die if he couldn't sink himself inside of her. If he couldn't feel her arching back, pressing her ass against him and silently forcing him to go deeper, to make the connection stronger.

A fool's errand, because how could they ever be more connected than they were every minute of every day?

He was still stroking her now-bare ass, and he slid his hand lower, teasing his way between her thighs. "Wider," he demanded, and she complied eagerly, not just spreading her legs, but bending over the back of the sexy little car so that she was wide open to him and just waiting to be fucked.

She still wore the silk blouse, and the image of the black top against the polished red car was so ridiculously sensual that he realized he'd stopped teasing her ass and was stroking his cock through the pants of his eight thousand dollar Kiton suit.

He bit the inside of his cheek, fighting the growing explosion inside him. *Not yet. Definitely not yet.* Instead, he set his hand to a more satisfying task, slowly stroking his wife from clit to ass and back again.

And oh, Christ, how he loved the way she responded. Her arms were splayed out, her head to the side so that her cheek was on the polished Bugatti. Her eyes were closed, and except for the hard-on-inducing way that she bit her lower lip, she wasn't moving above the waist at all, not even when she made the soft, sexy mewling sounds that never failed to drive him completely over the edge.

Below the waist was different. With each stroke, she rocked her ass in time with the movement of his hand. She wiggled her hips, too, as if silently begging him for more. And dear God she was wet.

He hadn't penetrated her yet, but his hand was wonderfully slick with the feel and scent of her. He lifted his fingers, unable to fight the urge to taste her, but he couldn't savor her sweetness because as soon as he lifted his hand away, she whimpered.

He was teasing her, no doubt about it, and God help him, he loved it. The way she moved. The way she responded. The sweet, desperate noises she made. He could stand there for eternity, his hands on her body, the scent of her arousal making him hard.

Slowly, he leaned over her, his middle finger sliding deep into her cunt as his thumb pressed against the flower of her ass. He brushed his lips over the curve of her ear. "Tell me you like that, baby."

"Yes," she murmured. "Oh, God, yes."

"Tell me you want more." He kissed his way down her neck to her collar, then pushed her hair aside with his mouth and kissed the back of her neck. The kisses were soft. Romantic, even. But the play of his fingers was not.

On the contrary, where his mouth teased her with gentle lips and soft kisses, his fingers tormented her with hard thrusts and naughty pleasures. "Touch yourself," he ordered as he thrust another finger into her sweet cunt. "Put your hand between your legs and play with your clit."

She complied eagerly, and when she moaned, he tugged his fingers free. "Take your hand away, too, baby."

"Damien, please." Her voice was low. Desperate. And the way she was writhing against her own fingers made him hard as steel.

He smacked her ass, relishing that sweet sting on his palm as she arched up, crying out with such wild abandon he thought he might come right then. "Disobeying?" Another spank, and then he cupped his hand on her hot bottom, rubbing gently as she finally pulled her hand free.

"What did you forget to say?"

For a moment she only breathed. "Yes, Sir." Her voice was strained, and he smiled as he slid his fingers back inside her, relishing the way she moved, fucking his hand and knowing she was pushing right up against the edge.

"That's my girl." He continued to rub her ass. "But someone forgot the rules."

"No, Sir. Please. Don't stop. I'll be good."

Christ, he loved this. Loved her. The way they played. The way she melted for him. Submitted to him. And her responses were all the more arousing because he knew damn well that one word from her could bring him to his knees.

He had the control? That was bullshit. She controlled his heart, his body, his soul. He was just along for the ride.

And it really was one hell of a ride.

"I know you will. Which is why I'll let you choose." He bent close, his palm resting gently on her rear. "Which do you want? My fingers in your cunt or my palm on your ass? Punishment or pleasure, baby? You tell me."

"No fair," she said. "It's a trick question."

"Is it?"

She turned her head, her eyes glazed with sensual heat. "With you, punishment is pleasure."

Her words filled his heart. "Baby," he said. "I think we'll have to go with both."

"Yes, please."

"Look forward, head down, and close your eyes."

She did as he ordered, and he slowly rubbed her ass cheek. "So beautiful. Do you have any idea how much I love marking you. Claiming you?"

"You don't have to claim me. I'm already yours."

"I know, baby. But I'm going to enjoy the privilege." He spanked her once, twice, then stroked her rear, soothing the sting before sliding his fingers between her cheeks and thrusting deep inside her core. She gasped, making small noises in her throat as she rocked against him, her body seeking to draw his fingers in deeper.

Again and again, until with the last spank, he teased her by sliding his sex-slick finger into her ass, desperate to take her completely over.

"Damien."

Need glazed her voice, slicing through his swirling, rapturous thoughts.

"Please," she begged. "Please fuck me. Now. Like that."

Hell, yes, he would. He didn't bother stripping. Just yanked down his fly and tugged his cock free. He was so fucking hard that the feel of his own hand almost made him explode, but he fought back, holding tight to the control he was famous for.

He slid his hands over her bare hip, then tugged her toward him, relishing her gasp as she slid along the back of the Bugatti until his cock was right at her center. He held her still, then entered her slowly until her demands that he go harder and deeper overwhelmed him and he pounded into her, his cock deep inside as he held her hip with one hand and teased her ass with the other, her cries of, "Yes, yes, oh, God, Damien, yes," echoing through the garage.

"Touch yourself, baby. I want you to come with me."

She didn't hesitate, and her fingers brushed his cock as she teased herself. Her body quivering and tightening around him as her release stormed down on her. He wanted to take her over, even as he wanted to keep her right there on the knife edge of a pleasure so intense it was almost like pain. An almost unendurable ecstasy of a kind he'd only ever felt with her, his wife, this woman who owned him completely.

"*Damien.*" His name was ripped from her as her body shuddered, passion filling her with such intensity it sent him spiraling over as well. He emptied himself into her, and felt his entire body go limp, completely sated, utterly satisfied.

He bent over, covering her body with his, and for a moment, they simply breathed. "Have I mentioned I love you?" he murmured when he'd recovered the power of speech.

"Once or twice. Here and there."

"I love you," he said again, because it really couldn't be said too many times.

"I love you, too. You're everything to me, Damien. You gave me the world when you gave me you."

He closed his eyes, reveling in those words, then gently kissed the back of her neck. "Don't move," he ordered, then eased off of her and went to the passenger side of the car. He found some tissues in the glove box, returned, and gently cleaned her up.

"Considering we both need to get to work, you should probably put your skirt back on."

"So conservative." She shot him a sexy smirk as she bent over for the skirt, then stepped into it, deftly buttoning it and sliding up the zipper. She adjusted her blouse, left her panties on the garage floor with a wink to him, then slipped on her shoes.

"I think we missed morning traffic," she said as she walked to the driver's side door, opened it, then slid into the car. She tossed him a look that was pure, sensual satisfaction.

"Get in, Mr. Stark. It's my turn to drive."

Chapter Eleven

"You sure you wouldn't rather I drive?" Damien asked as she slid to a stop in front of the drive-through window at Upper Crust.

"Nervous, Mr. Stark?"

"Terrified," he said dryly.

She just laughed and put her hand on his knee. "Until we get to my office, looks like I'm the one in charge."

"Be careful, Ms. Fairchild."

"Or else what?" Her voice was all innocence. "You'll punish me?" She leaned over so that her mouth was right at his ear, and she used her right hand on his upper thigh to balance. "Please, Mr. Stark," she whispered, her finger brushing his cock, which was rapidly getting into the spirit. "Please punish me."

He was tempted to pull her over to him, yank up her skirt, and spank her right there in the drive through. Instead, he said, "Hey, Kari," when the familiar manager appeared at the window with the order he'd texted in right as they'd left the garage.

"Oh, wow. It's great to see you guys. I'm so sorry about what happened, and I'm beyond glad Anne and Bree are okay. I saw the video, obviously. You got the muffins?"

"We did," Nikki said. "It was very thoughtful of you to send a basket. Thank you."

Kari passed the boxes into the car as Nikki handed her a credit card. "I still can't believe it was Rory. I mean, I introduced him to Bree. I'm the reason she started dating that nutcase. And nobody knew. Everyone said he was so normal. It's like this betrayal. All the regulars here—they all feel like family. But he was a wake-up call, I guess, because they're not." She shook her head and sighed. "Guess you can't be too careful."

"Do you remember how you met him?" Damien asked.

"Not really. He started coming once, twice a day. He'd sit and work. After a while, we talked. He was nice. Cute. Bree was single." She shrugged. "Honestly, I think I'm giving up matchmaking."

Behind them, someone in a silver Toyota honked.

"Really great to see you," Kari said, handing back the credit card along with their two coffees. "Be safe."

"She said to be safe," Damien said five minutes later as Nikki took the curves with a speed that defied physics. "I'm pretty sure you're walking on the wild side."

"With you? Always." But she slowed down, more because of the traffic congestion than because he'd complained. "What were the questions about? Does it matter how she met him? It's over, right? He confessed. He's being sentenced soon. It's done."

"Just curiosity," Damien said, because he heard the panic in her voice. And because he really was just curious. But that curiosity was fueled by a need to know everything about the man who snatched their daughter.

He leaned forward and pressed a button on the sound system. Immediately, the car filled with Dominion Gate, a Finnish heavy metal band that Jackson loved and that had performed live at Westerfield's, a Stark club in West Hollywood, on more than one occasion.

He sat back, enjoying both the music and the power of the car. And appreciating the way his wife handled the curves.

She glanced over at him, then turned down the volume. "You're far too comfortable. Shall I see if I can shave five minutes off the trip? Or heat up the morning even more?" she added, stroking his thigh.

"Eyes on the road, baby."

She squeezed his leg as they reached a red light. "You're not the only one who can multi-task."

"You are begging—*begging*—to be punished."

"Figured that out, did you?"

He laughed. A real, deep, full-on laugh. And damned if it didn't feel good.

She turned her head just long enough to smile at him. He saw the joy on her face, too, and they both knew what it meant. Healing. Thank

God, they really were healing.

"So why do you think Sofia called us both?" she asked as she turned left. "What's her agenda?"

"Maybe she doesn't have one," he said. "Maybe she just wants to ease into our lives now that she's well and life's settling back into a normal routine."

He glanced toward her, expecting a reply. Or at least a dubious snort. Instead, she just said, "This is my stop" as she pulled into a thirty-minute space in front of her building and killed the engine. "Are you coming up?"

"Absolutely. I need to see my wife's power center."

"Now you're just being kinky."

He glanced around. "On the sidewalk? I can be persuaded..."

Her lips twitched. "Stop it."

They were still laughing when they exited the elevator and entered the office. Nikki called a greeting to Marge, who currently doubled as both the receptionist and the office manager, but Damien stopped short, because he'd noticed the pixie-faced girl with deep brown eyes and strawberry blond curls.

"Hi," Sofia said, standing up from the chair.

Beside him, Nikki tightened her grip on his hand. "Sofia," she said. "You're here."

"I'm here. I—I wanted to talk. I didn't expect you, too," she said to him. "But I'm glad you're here."

"Oh." Nikki looked up at him, then back to Sofia. "Oh, I'm sorry. I'm being rude. I just didn't expect to see you. Marge, this is Sofia. She and Damien have known each other forever."

"Well, then it's a pleasure to meet you," the older lady said.

"Back at you."

"Come on," Nikki said. "We can go back to my office. Everyone else is probably in the conference room for the morning meeting." She shot Damien a sideways glance. "Unfortunately, I got here a little late."

She led the way, and Damien fell in step beside Sofia, grateful that Nikki had pulled herself together. They weren't BFFs by any means, but they'd made progress recently, and Damien had hope that his wife and his lifelong friend would ultimately reach a point where they would at least feel comfortable together.

"This is a really great space," Sofia said as they stepped into Nikki's corner office.

"It is," Nikki said. "And it's a lot better than it was the last time I saw it. Abby did a great job supervising the cleanup," she said to Damien. "And I know she had help. So thank you, too."

Sofia looked between the two of them. "What are you talking about?"

"Someone vandalized Nikki's office a few days before they were supposed to move in."

"Oh." Her nose wrinkled. "That's awful. What did they do?"

"Spray paint. Bullshit. I don't even want to think about it," Nikki said.

"I'm going to find out who did it," Damien told her. "That much I promise you."

"I believe you," Nikki said.

"You should," Sofia added. "When Damien says he'll do something, he does it. You can count on it."

"True enough," Nikki said, and when she smiled at Sofia, Damien thought he heard another chunk of ice melting away.

"So what's up, Sof?" Damien asked. "You called us both this morning but left no message."

Sofia lifted a shoulder, looking more like a little girl than a woman in her thirties. "I got these for the girls," she said, pulling two gift bags out of the giant tote she was carrying. "Just little stuffed animals, but since I didn't bring them before…"

She trailed off, and Damien took the bags with a simple "Thank you."

Sofia cleared her throat. "And, well, I wanted to say to Nikki that I saw the video. The one you did with Jamie. Talking about the kidnapping and how you cut."

"Oh." Nikki stiffened, which didn't surprise Damien. The blade she used that horrible day was one that Sofia had given to her years ago in a perverted attempt to force her to cut. Damien shuddered, imagining Nikki in her office that day, the antique scalpel in her trembling hand. And remembering only too well the way everything spun out of control in the days that followed.

"I just want to say that you should talk to someone. I mean, I did. And it really helped me. Maybe it'll help you, too."

Nikki's lips were pressed tight, and Damien reached over and took her hand. She held on—tight—but she nodded and said, "Thanks. I did talk to someone, and it did help. I really appreciate the concern. Truly."

"Good. I'm glad. You'll give the kids the presents?"

"Of course."

Damien squeezed Nikki's hand before releasing it, then moved to Sofia. "Come on. I'll walk you to the elevator."

"Right. Sure."

"Be right back," he said to Nikki, who nodded, looking only a little shell-shocked.

"Why are you really here?" he asked once they'd stepped out of the office and were standing in the elevator alcove.

"I—I don't know what you mean. I wanted to give Nikki the presents. And, um, tell her that talking to a counselor helps. That's all. Really. Was it bad for me to come?"

He considered the question. "Bad? No. But it wasn't good either."

She licked her lips. "I just want—Damien, I just want things to be right between us again. And that means I have to be okay with your wife. And, well, she has to be okay with me."

"And you thought that showing up unannounced was the way to do that? Coming to her office?" He kept his voice level. Gentle. "Sofia, honey, think about the last time you came to her office."

Her eyes widened so much she looked like a small animal caught in the headlights. "The last time?" Then she seemed to shake it off, leaving only sadness and understanding. "Oh," she said. "I wasn't thinking." She glanced back at the office doors. "Should I go apologize?"

He shook his head. "No. It'll be okay. But you need to give her space and time. We all want the same thing, truly. But it's going to take time and care. And that means no surprise visits. Okay? I need you to be patient. Can you do that?"

She nodded. "I can do whatever you need me to. If that's what it takes to make it right."

"Good. Thank you." He gave her a hug, hoping she truly understood, then put her on the elevator with a promise to call soon. Then he headed back into the office in time to run into Abby and Travis coming out of the conference room. The three of them made the hall crowded, and he watched Abby stiffen as Travis casually put a hand on her back to guide her out of the way.

"Hey, Mr. Stark," he said, pulling his hand away from Abby as if he'd been snakebit. "Nikki's first day back? How are you two doing?"

"We're okay," Damien said, remembering that Nikki had mentioned that she thought something was going on between Abby and Travis. All things considered, he thought she was right. "It's good to get back into a routine."

"Yes," Abby said. "It absolutely is. And speaking of routine, this is when I go through my emails."

She scurried off, and Travis shrugged. "She really does like things to be ordered."

"I'm guessing you go with the flow."

Travis just shrugged, but something about his grin suggested to Damien that there was a kernel of important truth hidden in there somewhere.

When he returned to Nikki's office, he found Eric with her. "Damien," he said. "Good to see you."

"You too." The former client development manager had left Fairchild Development to pursue an opportunity in New York, only to come back seeking his old job. Abby had done the hiring, and since Eric was standing right there, it was clear that she hadn't taken off too many points for his earlier defection.

"Listen," Eric said, "I wanted to thank you for believing me. About the graffiti, I mean."

"I didn't at first," Damien said. When he'd found Eric on-site right after Nikki had discovered the vandalism, he'd assumed the worst. Thankfully, he'd been wrong. And though he could dislike the man on principle for quitting on Nikki during prep for a major client, Damien couldn't fault a guy for following a business opportunity. Even if it inconvenienced his wife. "We're all good," he told Eric.

"I'm glad to hear it. And," Eric added, holding up his phone, "I have calls to make."

"Yes, you do. I want to know where our prototypes are," Nikki said.

"And I'm all over that. Later, Stark," he added before slipping out into the hallway.

Damien closed the door. "Looks like the wheels are still turning at Fairchild & Partners Development. Abby did a good job keeping the place going."

"She did great," Nikki agreed. "I feel almost useless."

"That's the point. Hire good people. Create a machine that drives itself. You're doing great, baby."

"That means a lot." A shadow darkened her eyes. "And I guess it means I could just cut out and go back home if I had to."

He gripped her upper arms and looked straight at her. "They're fine, Nikki. They're home. They're safe."

She nodded. "I know. It's just…"

"What?"

She licked her lips, then looked up at him. "Make me believe it?"

He saw it—the heat. The need. It was that spark that kept him sane. That kept the earth turning on its axis. She needed this—and so, goddammit, did he.

"Strip."

"What?" Her brows rose as if with shock, but the flare of desire in her eyes belied the expression of incredulity.

He kept his face stern, enjoying himself. "You heard me, Ms. Fairchild," he said as he moved to her door and locked it. "Everything. Off. Now."

Her teeth played over her lower lip, and he felt his cock grow hard in response.

"Didn't you just fuck me in the garage?"

"Arguing?"

"No, Sir."

He walked a circle around her. "First, I did fuck you in the garage, naked and spread out on the polished rear of my car. Second, I didn't say I was going to fuck you now. I told you to strip. And you're going to do just that. Aren't you?"

She nodded.

He took a step toward her, his skin seeming to vibrate from the electricity arcing between them. "You're mine, Nikki. Any time I want. Anywhere I say. So I'll say it again. Strip."

"Yes, Sir," she said, and he just about came right then from the knowledge that she wasn't doing this simply because he told her to, but because she enjoyed it, too.

The shoes came off first, followed by the skirt. He sucked in a breath—he'd forgotten about the panties that had been left behind. Then she unbuttoned the black silk blouse. She let it fall to the ground so that she stood in front of him in only a skimpy lace bra.

"That too. I want you bare. I don't think this office has been properly christened."

"No, it hasn't." Her voice was low. Breathy. Filled with desire.

"Tell me, baby. Do you like this? Naked in here with me. Your partner and employees just outside that door?"

"Yes."

"Touch yourself. Show me how much you like it."

She started to slide her hand between her legs, but he stopped her. "No. Get on the desk facing me. Spread your legs. And then feel how wet you are."

She didn't even hesitate, and she never took her eyes off of him. And when she spread her legs and stroked her sweet pussy—when she revealed all the scars that marred her beautiful thighs—he almost wept with joy. Because she didn't even pause. And those scars were once the thing she was most ashamed of.

"What toys do you have in your office?"

Her eyes, which had started to close in passion, went wide. "What—toys?"

God, he loved that he could still make her blush. "Let's start easy. Vibrator? Don't tell me you don't have one here." He stood and walked closer, then moved her hand aside so he could cup her heat. "Don't worry, baby. I like the idea of you working late, thinking about me, needing to get off fast and hard so that you can finish your work and get home so we can do it again, slow and easy."

"Oh." The word sounded strangled.

"I'll ask again. Toys?"

"Somewhere in that mess," she admitted, nodding toward a stack of boxes. "I—in a small lockbox tucked into a file box." She shrugged. "I haven't unpacked."

He was tempted to search. He'd only brought it up because he was curious, but once he'd pictured her in her chair, legs up on the desk, the rest of the office dark and locked as she got herself off and then cried his name...

Fuck.

"Slide to the edge," he ordered. "I can help you with this lack of toy problem." And then he knelt in front of her and kissed her inner thigh, his mouth moving slowly up the inside of one leg while his hand caressed the other. His thumb reached one of her scars, and he brushed the pad lightly over the hard, raised skin.

His mouth found the newest scar on her other thigh, and he traced his tongue lightly over it, hearing Nikki whimper. He didn't stop, didn't even hesitate. On the contrary, he moved his thumb higher, finding the hard button of her clit. He teased it with his finger as his tongue soothed the healing wound.

She sucked in air, her fingers twining in his hair and holding him in place. Her hips bucked in a silent demand that he not stop, and he knew that it was about more than the way he was stroking her clit, more even than her submission to his demands. It was understanding and consent, because she knew what he needed. What they both needed. Because this touch was important. It was his apology and his acquiescence. It was his acknowledgement of why she'd cut. And it was her silent assurance that she would never do it again.

Slowly, he teased his tongue up over the map of her scars, wishing he could have fought every one of her battles for her. Then he slipped his fingers deep inside her, moving slowly in and out as he sucked on her sweet, swollen clit.

She cried out, then clamped her mouth shut, obviously afraid that her coworkers would hear. Her body bucked, and her legs began to close, trapping him in heaven. He never faltered. He teased and tormented and pushed her to the edge until finally she arched back, her hips moving as she fucked his fingers, her core spasming around him, drawing him in as he relentlessly teased her clit until she couldn't take it any longer and she tugged on his hair to pull him back as the orgasm exploded through her, leaving her limp and flushed and breathing hard.

For a moment, he stayed on his knees, taking in the sight of the disheveled, naked woman perched on her desktop. Then he stood and casually took a business card from her silver cardholder. "Is this your card?"

She glanced at it, clearly confused, then nodded.

"A powerful woman," he said, moving to stand right in front of her. "A business owner. Yet I tell you to strip and you do. I tell you to fuck your fingers, and you would." He settled into the guest chair, then lowered his fly and took out his cock, once again as hard as steel. "I tell you to get on your knees and you will. Won't you, baby?"

"Oh, yes," she said. "I will."

"On your knees. Suck my cock."

She went down immediately, naked before him, her hands flat on her bare thighs.

"Do it," he said gently. "But first tell me why."

A thousand reasons she could give went through his head. Because she needed the submission. Because she knew he craved the control.

Because everything had spun out around them, and this was proof they hadn't lost who they were or what they meant to each other.

All true, and yet none entirely right.

Not until she spoke, and truth rang out between them.

"Because I love you, Mr. Stark. And," she added before she took his cock into her mouth, "because I'm yours."

Chapter Twelve

Because I love you, Mr. Stark. And because I'm yours.

His wife's words caressed Damien as he eased the Bugatti into traffic, heading toward the 10 and Stark Tower.

Simple, but so special, and so true. Words spoken not because of force or blackmail or bribery. Not because she was trading on his fame and power like some of the women he'd slept with in the pre-Nikki years.

No, she'd meant every word, every breath. Just as he loved her.

It might not be a perfect world, he thought as he accelerated onto the freeway, but there was some room for miracles. He knew, because he and Nikki had found each other.

Slowly, he stroked his cock. Not because he was looking to get off on the freeway, but because he wanted to savor the memory of what had been a truly spectacular morning blowjob. And not just his wife's skill with tongue and lips and hands, but the way she'd looked. Naked and beautiful and strong. Strong enough to bring him to his knees, that was for damn sure.

And she *was* strong. Stronger than she believed she was. And strong enough to hand him control when he needed it.

Having a woman like that at his side … well, that was powerful stuff. Maybe he'd had to wait those six long years for her, but never could he say that it wasn't worth the wait.

Hell, she even put up with the ghosts of his childhood for him. Because she understood that it was important to him. That so long as Sofia was trying to help herself, then Damien wanted—no, *needed*—to help her, too. They'd endured too much together, and that kind of suffering forged an unbreakable bond.

Not that he'd imagined the depth of their torment when he'd first seen her. No, the first time he'd met Sofia, she was simply his hard-driving new coach's pretty daughter. She'd sit in the stands and read while Damien practiced, and after, she'd tell him he did great.

Coach Richter blew hot and cold about their growing friendship, some days seeming not to care, some days teasing that they'd grow up and get married, some days telling Sofia to stay away so she didn't knock Damien off his game.

It was easier when Alaine eased in and made their twosome a threesome. Richter still pushed Damien hard on the court, but after games and practice, he was less rigid. Alaine and Sofia and Damien had the chance to enjoy rare free time. The son of the sports doctor, Alaine was homeschooled and often traveled on the same schedule as Damien, and the three became fast friends.

Then things changed.

In the Bugatti, he tightened his hands on the wheel, grateful to have reached his exit. He needed the distraction of traffic lights and turns as those memories flooded his mind. The way Richter would pull him aside in the shower. The unwelcome touches. The bold move of taking Damien out of the dorms and giving him his own room. One to which Richter had a key.

Those nights were bad enough. That vile creature touching him. Talking to him. Breathing near him. But then Damien would come home to find Sofia there. Or Sofia and Richter. And Richter always had his camera.

Damien shuddered as he whipped the steering wheel to the right, barely making the turn into the Stark Tower garage. He took the turns too fast, then barreled into his parking slot, barely slamming on the brakes in time to keep from crumpling the Bugatti's front end.

He'd been there.

Watching. Directing. Telling Damien how to touch her. *Where* to touch her. Telling Sofia how to stroke his cock. Telling her not to stop even though Damien wasn't hard. Because he would be—eventually, he would be.

And then, to his shame, Richter's prediction had been right. And Richter told him to put it in Sofia. Because if he didn't things would get very bad. He had pictures, after all. But he couldn't—he just couldn't do it. Not to Sofia. And he got soft, and he thought that Richter would stop. But instead Richter used his hand—*oh, holy Christ, Damien had wanted to die*—to make him hard, and had kept him that way with a black circle of rubber. A cock ring, he'd later learned.

And he'd made Damien fuck her, and she'd whispered that it was okay. Even begged him to do it. *Because if you don't, he'll punish me later.* And so Damien had. And he hadn't cried until they'd left his room.

And he'd promised himself that no matter what, he would always—*always*—protect Sofia. Because her father sure as hell wasn't going to.

In the Bugatti, Damien pounded his fist against the steering wheel.

He regretted nothing—*nothing*—about Richter's death except that if he had to do it all over again, he wouldn't have simply stood back and watched as Richter's handhold slipped and he fell to his death. No, in a do-over, Damien wouldn't hesitate to push the abusive fuck right over the edge.

So yeah, maybe Sofia had her issues. No big surprise there. God knew Damien had a cargo plane full of his own. But she was still his. Not the same way Nikki was—not even close. But Sofia was his responsibility. More, she was his friend. They'd come through hell, and if that didn't fuse two people together for life, Damien didn't know what did.

And though Damien had drawn the line and cut all contact with Sofia when she'd gone completely off the rails, he'd been beyond grateful when her doctors had said she'd recovered. She was fragile, yes. But she was better.

And even though he knew it was difficult for Nikki, Damien was glad to have his friend back. And even more glad that his wife understood why.

Slowly, he drew in three deep breaths, forcing all of that shit out of his head. He didn't need it there. Not today. Not when he needed to be the man who ate billion dollar deals for breakfast.

Although...

He hadn't yet killed the Bugatti's engine, and now he used the voice command to dial Alaine's number. His friend answered on the first ring, speaking English with the kind of accent acquired from living all over Europe...and then settling in Santa Monica to become a world-renowned chef.

"I feel terrible that you have called first, my friend. I keep wanting to check in about little Anne, but I did not want to interrupt your family time."

"Appreciated," Damien said. "Actually, today's the first day that Nikki and I have gone back."

"I'm glad you are healing, and that the little one is well?"

"She is. She doesn't remember a thing."

"That is a blessing."

"A huge one. Listen, Alaine, I don't have much time, but I wanted to see if you could come to the house for brunch on Sunday. Not a big party. In fact, Nikki's going to be out with a friend. It would just be you, me, Sofia, and my girls. I thought that it would be nice to reconnect. And be relatively drama free about it."

"Sofia is in town? How did I not know this?"

"She had a rough time recently. A miscarriage. I'm probably speaking out of turn, but you know how she is. I don't want the subject of pregnancy to come up, and—"

"Of course, of course. I am the very face of discretion."

"I'll check with Sofia, but unless she has a conflict, we'll see you Sunday at ten."

"I look forward to it."

Damien ended the call, then nodded. This felt good. Like he was moving forward. *Healing.*

He thought about what Nikki said after she'd met with the counselor earlier in the week. She'd come back and told him that it had helped. That healing had to be active, and you couldn't just sit back and wait for scabs to form over all the raw places.

Possibly not the best analogy considering she'd drawn blood, but he agreed with the sentiment.

He had one more call to make, and he listened to the robotic ringtone until the line clicked, and he heard Orlando McKee's throaty voice say, "Nikki?"

"No, it's Damien. Just like your phone says."

"Is Nikki okay?" he asked, and the urgent, obviously sincere worry caused his stock to rise another notch in Damien's book.

"Nikki's fine. It's her first day back at work, and I thought she might enjoy some time with you and Jamie tonight. One of your all-night wine and movie parties. Whatever you three want."

"Uh-huh. Us three?"

Damien rubbed his temples, amused. He could picture Ollie pushing his glasses up his nose, his brow furrowed in confusion, his longish hair pulled back in a man bun which, surprisingly didn't look ridiculous. "I'm trying to do a nice thing here, McKee," he said. "Nikki hasn't had nearly enough time with her best friends."

He waited for Ollie to protest that he and Nikki had grown apart. That things had changed when she'd married Damien.

Instead, he just said, "Yeah. Not nearly enough time."

"I thought about having Edward drive you all to the Arrowhead house—or wherever you decide. Or offer you the Tower Apartment. But I honestly don't think Nikki wants to get that far away from the girls yet."

"No, probably not. You're really setting this up just for the three of us?"

Damien ignored him. "Now I'm thinking the bungalow. It's already stocked, you have the beach, it's away from the main house, but she can get to the girls in minutes if she needs or wants to. Which she won't, because I'll undoubtedly be occupied by my own Disney marathon. Hopefully without a puppy in sight. But confidence is low."

"Um, yeah. Listen, man, this sounds great. Thank you."

"My pleasure. How does eight sound? And I need to get up to the office. Could you call and run all this by Jamie?"

"Eight sounds terrific, and of course."

"Great. I'll tell Nikki. Pop in and say hi or just head straight to the bungalow. Your call."

"Okay. Will do."

He still sounded a little baffled, a fact that amused Damien. And was somewhat gratifying, too. In the cutthroat world of buying and selling the universe, it was handy to have a reputation as a major badass.

"I gotta say, Stark. Every once in a while, you surprise me."

Damien grinned, thinking of Ollie's recent confession that he'd been secretly working for the FBI. "Yeah, McKee. I know the feeling."

Chapter Thirteen

"I appreciate you seeing me," Richard Breckenridge said, as Damien's assistant, Rachel Peters, led him into the office near the end of the workday, then excused herself.

Damien remained seated behind his desk while Jackson stood at the window, a commanding presence in a gray tailored suit. He didn't turn to greet Breckenridge. Just stayed as he was, looking casually out at downtown LA, fifty-seven stories below.

Normally, Damien would stand and shake a guest's hand. And for most afternoon meetings, they'd settle onto the couch or chairs in the seating area near the front of the huge office. Enjoy coffee or bourbon and converse like friends about whatever business matter was the order of the day.

Richard Breckenridge, however, was neither a friend nor a respected colleague. And as far as Damien was concerned, this meeting wasn't about building a relationship. It was about assessing Breckenridge. More than that, it was about making absolutely clear who was in charge.

And that would be Damien.

To underscore the point, he gestured to one of the guest chairs on the far side of his massive desk. Then he leaned back casually, resting his head in his intertwined fingers. "I've got a window of fifteen minutes before my next meeting. Why don't you tell me why we're sitting here, Richard?"

Breckenridge shifted, the hard planes of his face forming into a frown. This wasn't the way meetings between two players in the corporate world usually began. This was how a meeting with an incompetent subordinate might begin.

Damien stayed relaxed, watching his guest. In his peripheral vision, he saw Jackson turn so that he was now casually leaning against the floor to ceiling windows, protected from a deadly fall by nothing more than a few centimeters of glass. He seemed utterly unconcerned, however. Instead, his focus was entirely on Breckenridge, and Damien had to fight to keep back a smug grin. He'd been on the receiving end of that deadly, icy stare. And though he'd come out unscathed, Damien knew just how formidable Jackson could be.

Between the two brothers, this meeting was definitely not going to be a cakewalk for Breckenridge. And Damien considered that a damn good thing.

"I heard about what happened to your daughter," Breckenridge said, his pale gray eyes as cold as slate. "I was very relieved to hear that she's come through the ordeal so well. You and your wife must have been terrified. Please give her my regards."

"I appreciate the good thoughts, Richard. But I don't think I'll be mentioning your name to my wife." He turned the chair so that he could catch Jackson's eye. "You know Nikki. Do you think she'd want condolences from a man who says the kind of things that my guest here said to her?"

"I don't imagine any woman wants well-wishes from a man who called her a whore." Jackson shrugged casually. "Better to stay silent and not ruin her day."

"Exactly my thought," Damien said. "Thanks."

"Anytime, brother."

Damien watched as a muscle in Breckenridge's cheek twitched and his hands gripped the leather armrests so tightly his knuckles turned white. "I was upset," he said evenly. "I spoke without thinking. And as I mentioned to your assistant, I had hoped to see your wife today to give her my apology in person."

"I'll deliver that for you. As I believe we've established, you're not anyone she needs to see or talk to."

"Damien—"

"I think we'll stick with Mr. Stark. Okay by you, Richard?"

Breckenridge said nothing.

"Now why don't you tell me just how upset you were the day you spoke to my wife that way?"

The other man's brow furrowed. "What the hell are you talking about, Stark?"

Damien raised a brow and said nothing.

"*Mister* Stark," Breckenridge said grudgingly.

Damien pressed one of the recessed control buttons on his desktop. The glass in the windows darkened and the overhead lights dimmed. At the same time, a screen dropped from the ceiling on the far side of the room, just over the wet bar. A recessed projector descended from the ceiling, and an image flashed onto the screen. "*That's* what I'm talking about."

Breckenridge turned, his eyes going wide as he looked at the image of Nikki's office. The red Xs spray-painted over the walls and blinds. And the word BITCH standing out in the center of it all.

"I didn't—you really think I had something to do with this?"

"I did," Damien admitted. "Watching you now, I'm inclined to change my opinion." He glanced at Jackson, saw his brother nod in agreement. Whatever else Breckenridge might be, he wasn't their vandal. Unless, of course, he was the world's best actor.

"Good," Breckenridge said, and Damien could practically see the confidence flowing back into the man. "That's good to hear. Because I'd like us to start fresh."

"Fresh?"

"With The Domino," he said, looking from Damien to Jackson and then back to Damien again. "My company is an asset, Mr. Stark. Mr. Steele. You both know that. It's why you wanted me as one of the original tenants. And God knows my investment helped move the project along."

"Your investment was returned to you, with a significant negotiated percentage to compensate for any inconvenience. If you have a problem with the terms, I suggest you have your attorney contact Mr. Maynard," Damien added, referring to his long-time counsel, Charles Maynard.

"Of course. I mean, no. I don't have a problem with the terms. I should have said *re*-investment. I want back in."

"I don't see that happening," Damien said. "And as for the company, I think The Domino will do just fine without having Breckenridge Tech as an anchor tenant."

"So you're going to keep me out why? Because of spite? You realize that punishing me punishes your father. That man's in debt to me for a cool two mil. He was going to make that and more from The Domino, and we all know it."

"That's right," Jackson said to Damien. "Jeremiah invested with Richard here so that Richard could invest in The Domino."

"Yes, yes, exactly," Breckenridge said, latching onto Jackson's use of his given name as if it were a sign from God that they were destined to be best friends. "I agreed to extend the deadline for the two mil he owes me so that he could invest his liquid assets in his sons' extraordinary venture through me. Shut me out and you shut him down, too. Or don't either of you care about that?"

"If you did your homework, I think you'd know I don't care about that at all." Damien swiveled in his chair so he could look straight at Jackson. "How about you? Any niggles of conscious about our father's current financial state?"

Jackson's mouth curved into a thoughtful frown, and he shook his head. "No. Not a care in the world."

"Sorry, Richard," Damien said. "Looks like you're dealing with two heartless bastards. Pity."

"You know, dear old Dad should probably take better care about who he invests with," Jackson said.

Richard's face contorted into a snarl as he shot to his feet. "And I'm thinking you two should have thought better about cutting me out for nothing more than the accusations of a few frustrated bitches."

"On the contrary, I think we made the exact right move. Jackson? Any remorse on clearing the garbage out of the project?"

"I'm feeling pretty good about it."

"You're both son-of-bitches, you know that?" He leaned forward, his palms flat on the desktop as he looked Damien hard in the eyes. "You really going to tell me no woman's ever said you came on too strong?"

Damien didn't flinch, didn't blink. "I've been accused of a lot of things, but never of rape. Or battery. Or of demanding sex in exchange for a promotion, and then taking what I wanted by force if she had the balls to say no, or destroying her career if she managed to get out of my office unscathed. Unlike you, Richard, I'm a full-fledged supporter of the concepts of *no* and consent."

"Well, I hope you never have to face the kind of trumped-up furor I'm dealing with. Hell of a thing to stomach when it's not true."

"I'm sure it would be very traumatic—to a man who's innocent. *No*—" He held up a hand, forestalling Breckenridge's next rant. "Do you think we didn't do our due diligence before removing you? We talked to every one of the women who've gone public."

"And at least a dozen more who stayed quiet," Jackson added. "Not true? The hell it's not."

"And even if we'd never talked to a single one of those women, considering what you said to my wife, I'd be a little hesitant to take you on faith."

"You're going to regret this. Do you think I don't know about you? Do you think that compared to me you have clean hands? Your dad pimped you out for money and fame. He fucked you up, and we both know it. You killed Merle Richter, Stark, and the only reason you're not rotting in a German jail is that he was a perverted worm."

"Careful," Jackson said, his voice low and dangerous.

"Or you'll do what, Steele? Bloody me? You think I don't know about *your* crimes and misdemeanors? Everything that went on in Santa Fe? The people you hurt to keep that tell-all movie off the screen?"

Damien met Jackson's eyes, saw the heat building on his brother's face. He didn't know all of it, but he knew Jackson's temper matched his own. And he also knew that Jackson had done what was necessary to shield his daughter, Veronica, from the prying eyes of the press.

"If you know that," Jackson told Breckenridge, "then you know that it isn't wise to push my buttons. Mine or my brother's."

"Fuck you both," Breckenridge said. "I know enough to bury you."

"Then try." Damien pushed back his chair and stood up, looking down at the man still resting his greasy palms on Damien's desk. "But right now, I want you out of my office, you sniveling, misogynistic fuck."

Chapter Fourteen

"Well, that was bracing," Jackson said later as he kicked back on the leather sofa in Damien's sitting area. "It's almost four. Too early for something stronger than coffee?"

"Tempting," Damien said, pouring himself a cup from the carafe Rachel had left on the sidebar. "I think I'll save the hard stuff for after my next appointment."

"Christ, that's right. You're seeing Claymore in a bit."

"We are," Damien confirmed. "I'd appreciate it if you and Sylvia would come, too. If you can get away. I know Nikki would like—*we* would like—to be with family."

Jackson didn't answer. Instead, he leaned over and pushed the intercom button on the phone next to the sofa. "Yes, Mr. Stark?"

"Steele, actually. Could you call down to my office and have them clear the rest of my day. And ask Sylvia to do the same then meet me up here. Tell her it's important."

"Of course, Mr. Steele," she said, her voice tinny through the speaker.

Jackson leaned back, and without missing a beat, said, "So why do you think the jackass wants to see you?"

Damien met his brother's eyes in a silent thank you, then settled into the chair across from him. "Absolution, I'm guessing."

"Will he get it?"

Damien looked at Jackson's face, so like his own. Hard lines and angles and eyes that missed nothing. "What do you think?"

"Hell, no."

Jackson nodded slowly. "Jeremiah called me after the girls' party.

Well, he called Sylvia. Probably assumed I wouldn't be interested in taking his calls. He was right, but I wasn't going to make my wife suffer for it, so I spoke to him."

The shift in conversation didn't surprise Damien. They were talking about absolution, after all. And neither of Jeremiah's sons felt particularly forgiving to their father. "What did he want?"

"Said he was concerned about Anne. I guess he heard about it on the news. He wanted to know if he should call you."

"No."

"And that's what I told him."

Damien nodded, then looked at his coffee. "Maybe it's time for a drink after all."

"I wouldn't say no."

He crossed the room to the wet bar, then returned with a half-full bottle of 25-year Macallan and two glasses. He poured, then handed one to Jackson, whose brows rose. "Nice to know I rate the good stuff."

The words were light, but Damien heard the truth behind them. That Jackson was just as glad as Damien that they'd overcome the past thrust upon them by their father.

He lifted his glass. "To family," he said. "The kind that's forged from more than blood."

"I'll drink to that."

He was still enjoying the smooth burn of that first incredible sip when Rachel's voice sang out over the intercom. "Your father-in-law is here. He doesn't have an appointment, but he asked if you could spare a few moments?"

"Of course," Damien said, then rose when the door opened to greet the older man, who had a kind but weathered face, brown hair that had gone gray at the temples, and eyes that telegraphed that he was Nikki's father. "Frank, it's good to see you. Drink?"

"Yeah, thanks. I could use it." A travel photographer, Frank wore khaki pants, an army green T-shirt, and a utility vest full of pockets. Two cameras hung from straps around his neck. He shoved his hands into his pockets, his weight shifting from foot to foot.

Damien gestured to a chair as he crossed the room for a fresh glass.

"Good to see you again," Jackson said. "Should I get out of your hair?"

"What? Oh, no. No. I was just taking some postcard shots of

downtown LA. Always a good seller at stock sites. Figured I'd drop in. Say hi to my son-in-law. Consider yourself a bonus, Jackson."

Jackson laughed. "I'm flattered."

Frank took the glass Damien handed him, then settled into a chair. "And I, uh, wanted to check in. Make sure you and Nikki are doing okay after ... everything. And Anne." His throat moved as he swallowed. "I wanted to check in on Anne, too."

Such a difference, Damien thought. He didn't believe in Jeremiah's motives for calling Jackson about Anne at all. But Frank...

Well, he was dead certain that Frank was ripped up inside. Not just because of the trauma that had happened to the people he loved, but also because he knew that he'd botched the handling of it completely.

He'd come here today to prostrate himself before Damien in silent apology for that failure. And Damien respected the hell out of him for it.

"She's doing well," he said gently, intentionally being vague about which Stark female he was talking about.

Frank met his eyes, then nodded, his lips tight with suppressed emotion. "Thank you." Though almost inaudible, it was clear the words were heartfelt.

"She's avoiding me, you know," Frank said. "She hasn't returned my call. I know—" He looked between Jackson and Damien. "I just...I mean, I never—I guess I never figured out how to be a father."

"I'm not sure you ever do," Jackson said. "You just do the best you can."

"I don't want to make it worse for her. With her mother..."

Damien flashed a wry grin. "I understand. But you're not Elizabeth. As long as you're there for Nikki—and you're genuine—you'll do just fine."

Frank put his drink on the table in front of him, then bent over, his elbows on his knees and his head in his hands. "I didn't mean to hurt her. That was the last thing I wanted. But damned if I didn't mess everything up."

Damien saw the signal light flash above the door. "I think she's the one you need to tell."

"Don't I know it."

"And," Damien added, standing as the door opened and Nikki stepped in, "I think now's the perfect time."

He watched as Nikki's brows rose. "Perfect time for what—*oh*.

Dad—I mean, Frank. I didn't realize you were here."

Frank was standing now, his hands shoved into his pants' pockets. "I came to see Damien. I thought he might have advice."

"Business advice?"

"Ah, no. Actually, I was looking for guidance on how to claw my way out of the doghouse."

"Apparently, your father thinks I have some experience with that."

As he'd hoped, she laughed. "Not that much," she said, coming up beside him and hooking her arm through his. "But if Damien told you to say that, I think he's given you some good, solid advice. And," she added with a tentative smile, "I think the fact that you came to ask was a good first step."

It was as if her words worked magic, eviscerating the layer of anxiety that had wrapped around Frank like a cloak, so palpable that Damien could see every fold and crease.

"We should talk," he said. "Do you think we could sit down and talk? Maybe we can go grab a drink at the Biltmore," he added, referring to the hotel down the hill from Stark Tower.

"I'd love that," she said, "but we have to go to the prison."

On the sofa, Jackson chuckled. "If I had a dime for every time someone used that excuse with me..."

Nikki rolled her eyes. "Rory—you know, the guy who took Anne—wants to talk to us."

"Why?"

"That's the question of the day," Damien said.

"Why don't you come?"

"Oh, no," Frank said. "I don't want to intrude."

"You're not," she assured him. "You're family."

"Jackson and Sylvia are coming, too," Damien added, earning a smile from Nikki after she noted Jackson's nod in acknowledgement.

"Oh. Well. I don't know." Frank shifted on his feet, and Damien recalled Frank's earlier words—*I never figured out how to be a father.*

"It would mean a lot if you come," Nikki urged.

Damien drew in a breath, afraid that Nikki was about to be deeply disappointed.

But then Frank nodded. "Of course, sweetheart. Of course I'll come."

＊ ＊ ＊ ＊

The interview room was small and shabby, with an odor that recalled to Damien the scent of the showers in some of the more poorly maintained tennis centers he'd visited in his youth. Three walls were solid. The fourth contained a large picture window concealed by a set of dusty venetian blinds. At the moment, the door was open, which reduced some, but not all, of the claustrophobic atmosphere.

"Well, it's definitely not Stark Tower," Frank said, earning a smile from everyone, if not a downright laugh.

Jackson and Sylvia sat at the long, scarred conference table, the metal chairs squeaking with every movement. He had his arm around her, and she was snuggled against him, her dark brown hair tousled.

Damien leaned against the wall in the far back corner, his eyes on his wife, who paced the length of the table opposite Jackson and Syl.

"Baby," he said, holding out his hand for her. She came, gave his hand a squeeze, then started pacing again.

"Sorry. I'm sorry. I just can't stand still." She looked up at the clock mounted on the wall, then checked the time on her phone's lock screen. "We've been here almost fifteen minutes. What's going on?" She glanced at Frank. "Something's wrong. Nobody ever makes Damien wait," she added, making Jackson burst out laughing.

"Sorry," he said. "But your wife has a point."

"It's true," Syl added. "I worked his desk for years. I can attest that my husband speaks the truth."

In the middle of the room, Nikki rolled her eyes. "Sorry. Honestly, I'm sorry. I'm just—I want to know why we're even here."

Damien took a step toward her, but paused when Frank hooked an arm around her shoulder, pulling her close. His throat tightened, and he had to swallow a knot of melancholy. Because no matter how much Frank had screwed up, he'd earned his way back. Something Damien knew damn well Jeremiah would never do.

With her head on her father's shoulder, she looked at Damien. "Seriously. Any ideas?"

"They're probably waiting for Charles. I think prison types like an attorney in the room."

"Well, where is he?" Sylvia asked.

"I don't know. He texted that he was parking right as they showed us back here. Haven't heard a word since. And yes," he said in response to his wife's upcoming question, "I've been trying to reach him."

She made a face, but said nothing. Just pushed a lock of hair out of her eyes and then led her father to the table. "Might as well sit."

"We'll know something soon," Frank said.

"I think we'll know it now," Jackson said. "Listen."

Sure enough, footsteps sounded in the previously quiet hallway. A moment later, two men in suits and ID badges that marked them as employees of the prison walked in, with Charles Maynard striding along in front of them.

Damien's attorney since his tennis days, Charles was a brilliant litigator, a shark in negotiations, and he never lost his shit when it counted.

At the moment, he looked decidedly flustered.

Fuck.

"What's going on?" Nikki asked before Damien got the words out.

"Have a seat." Charles nodded to a chair. And since Damien was the only one still standing, he knew the comment was for him. He continued to stand.

Charles sighed. "Have it your way."

"Dammit, Charles," Nikki said. "What is it? Where's Rory Claymore?" She was talking to Charles, but she was looking to Damien, clearly wondering why he wasn't the one who'd taken point on asking the questions.

But Damien had seen the badges. The Custody Investigative Services Unit. And that told him everything he needed to know.

"Claymore's not coming," Damien told her gently. "I'm guessing he's dead."

Chapter Fifteen

The investigators laid it all out, their words confirming what Damien already suspected—Rory Claymore was dead.

"How?" Nikki asked.

The taller of the two investigators shook his head. "Shivved. Kidneys, throat, heart. The attack took place an hour ago in the exercise yard."

"Then it was specific to Claymore," Damien said. "He didn't get caught up in a prison fight."

"No, sir. Someone clearly targeted him."

"You have a suspect?" Charles asked.

"Not at this time," the shorter man said.

"How can that be?" Nikki asked, taking Damien's hand in her own. "It's a prison. These men are watched all the time."

"They're locked up all the time," Sylvia said gently. "Not watched. When my dad—" Her voice broke. "Well, he's told me that a lot of time it's anything goes."

Nikki's hand tightened in Damien's, but she said nothing. Just nodded acquiescence.

"I assure you we're taking the investigation seriously, and when we have a suspect we'll let you know."

"But, well—" Nikki met Damien's eyes, and he stepped in, asking the question for her.

"Did Rory speak to anyone here about why he wanted to meet with us?"

"Not that we're aware. When the meeting was scheduled, he asked that it be confidential."

"We think there was a leak," the second investigator said. "By the time we reached the body, the inmates were buzzing with the news that he was meeting with Damien Stark today. Considering he wanted it confidential, I don't think Claymore was the one who shared that bit of intel."

Damien looked at Charles and saw that his attorney was wondering the same thing—what did someone not want Damien to know?

"Maybe nothing," Charles said later as they stood outside the prison.

"I doubt that," Jackson said. "Way too coincidental. And I don't believe in coincidences."

"Honestly," Charles said, his voice weary, "neither do I."

Damien looked between his brother and his lawyer. "We're going to find out. Who killed him—and why. And I don't mean who stabbed him," he clarified. "I'm talking about the person outside the prison pulling the strings. Because the only reason to keep Rory Claymore from talking to us today was to keep him from disclosing information about Anne's kidnapping."

Nikki's hand tightened in his. She looked up at him, fire in her eyes. "And the only person who'd care if he talked would be someone he was working with."

"Call Ryan," Damien ordered, his attention on Charles. "Explain the situation. Get him set up at the house with a team."

"Command central all over again." Fear colored Nikki's voice.

A raw, primal anger flooded his gut, and he pulled her to him, his hands cupping her face. "We're going to find the son-of-a-bitch, baby. That's a promise."

* * * *

Nikki was quiet during the drive home, and Damien didn't push her. He was processing it, too, after all. Instead, he tried to silently convey both strength and the certainty that they would find out who was behind Claymore's death ... and Anne's kidnapping.

She was still silent when he pulled into the circular drive in front of the house, eschewing the garage for the sake of expedience. The others were already there, and the sooner Damien could get to them, the sooner they could begin the briefing.

But first, he needed to check on his wife. He killed the engine, then took her hand. "Talk to me. Are you okay?"

She nodded, her brow furrowing as she turned to look at him. "I thought you arranged it."

He shook his head, not following her line of thought.

"When that investigator confirmed what you said—that Rory was dead, I mean—that's what I thought. That you'd arranged it somehow. Pulled strings. Paid someone off." She licked her lips. "I did, Damien. I thought it was you, and you'd had him killed for what he did to Anne."

His chest had been tightening as she talked, and now he realized he'd been holding his breath. "It wasn't me."

Her throat moved, her lips parting. Then she pulled her hand free and rubbed her palms on her skirt. "I know. I realized in the room, when we were talking with the investigators. Watching you, I mean. I could tell it wasn't you. But, Damien," she added, turning haunted eyes on him, "part of me really wishes it was."

She held his eyes for only a split second before looking back down at her hands twisting in her lap. "I wanted you to have killed him. I did. It wasn't revulsion I felt when I thought that you had. It was joy." She blinked up at him. "Fear, too. But only because I was afraid you'd get caught. I'm sorry."

"No," he said, cupping her neck, then pulling her close and kissing her sweetly. "Oh, baby, no. I thought the same thing. That I wished it had been me. That I'd taken that step and taken him out."

He brushed the pad of his thumb over her cheekbone. "I thought about it. I really did. After we caught him. After they took him away and he was no longer there in front of me. No longer a man I could demand answers from. No longer where I could reach him. Where I could get retribution."

With a low groan of frustration, he dragged his fingers through his hair. "So yeah, I thought about it. And baby, I'm sure I could have managed it. But then I thought harder. And I knew that if I did pull those strings, it might come back to me. And if that happened, I could end up in prison. I could lose you. The girls."

A shudder cut through him, and Nikki grabbed his hands, pressing them to her heart. "I came close to that in Germany. Prison. Losing you. And I watched Jackson come even closer. Close enough that the shadow of prison bars marked him, and he almost lost Sylvia. Ronnie. I watched what he went through in those days, and thought I might die if I lost you like that. I couldn't, baby. Not even to destroy the man who took Anne."

"I know." Tears hung on her lashes. "I'm glad he's dead. And I can imagine the feel of my hands around his throat. But I'm glad it wasn't either one of us. Because I couldn't bear losing you, either."

He brushed his thumb over her lower lip and smiled gently. "Then I guess it's good that someone else had the idea."

"Except it's not."

"No," he agreed, sobering. "It's not."

"You really think that's what it means?" she asked. "That someone else was involved."

"Don't you?"

She nodded. "Yeah. I do."

"And more than that—now I'm thinking Rory was just a pawn. Which means we still don't know who was really behind the kidnapping. But we will, sweetheart. I promise, we will."

* * * *

"The trouble," Charles said, "is that we can't prove why he was killed. We can speculate, but that's not proof. And without proof, we're not going to be able to get the LAPD interested in diving into a kidnapping case when the child is no longer in danger. For all we know, someone in prison gutted the son-of-a-bitch for snatching a little girl. There are codes. Even in prison."

"There may be, but we all know that wasn't what happened," Damien said. They were all seated at the massive equipment-covered conference table that now dominated the third floor open area, the area that was usually the heart of their home. Now, it was command central again, just as it had been during Anne's kidnapping.

The full team would arrive in the morning, a group hand-picked by Ryan for their field and tech skills. A smaller group, since it wasn't an active kidnapping. But sharp, talented people.

Damien had to hand it to Ryan—he'd pulled everything together, people and equipment, in record time.

From his spot at the head of the table, Ryan stood, tall and lean and in full command. He looked at the men in the room, his blue eyes landing on everyone in turn. "This isn't a liability. Without official involvement, we can move more freely. Once we have proof, we can bring in the authorities." He glanced at Damien, who nodded in agreement.

Quincy Radcliffe leaned back in the office-style chair that had been brought in with the rest of the equipment. A British agent with MI6 who did some off-the-books intelligence work in the States, Quincy looked the part. He had a lean, rugged face, a competent manner, and just a hint of mystery. Not to mention the James Bond accent.

Damien had respected him from the moment they'd met, and trust hadn't been far behind.

"The prison officials will let us know if they get a lead on the wanker who gutted Claymore," Quincy said, "but we can't count on that. Which means that we need to go back to where we left off before Rory was captured."

"You mean the suspects you were looking at before you captured Rory." Ollie spoke up from where he stood, leaning casually against the wall. Damien had forgotten all about inviting him and Jamie over, and the two had been in the house when he'd arrived, having come up from the bungalow after Ryan called Jamie, his wife, to bring her up to speed. Now, Jamie was with Nikki, Sylvia, and Bree, getting the girls ready for bed. Ollie had insisted on staying with the team, and considering his FBI connections, Damien was glad for the help. "Glad I got cleared off that red letter suspect list," Ollie added with a wry grin.

"Had to be thorough," Damien countered. "Besides, you were an ass when Nikki and I first got together. Consider it payback."

"*I* was the ass?" Ollie retorted. And, as Damien had hoped, they both laughed. Ollie might never be on Damien's top ten list, but he knew that Orlando McKee would move the world for Nikki. And if for no other reason, that meant that Damien would do whatever necessary to build a bridge.

Now, Ollie looked at Quincy. "So back to the beginning, you said. But where exactly does that put us?"

"The money and the players."

Ryan nodded. "Before Rory popped up like a rabid groundhog, we were looking at Breckenridge and Jeremiah."

"I'd love to squash Breckenridge like a bug," Jackson said, "but if he's behind this kidnapping, the man has balls of steel." He turned to

Damien. "He practically begged to be let back into The Domino. Hell of a risk. He says one thing he shouldn't, one offhand comment, and he has to know that you'd make sure that hell rained down on him."

"It's a point," Charles said. "But that leaves Jeremiah. Do we really believe that he could do that to his own grandchildren?"

"Have you forgotten what he did to me?" Damien snapped, then immediately regretted it. "Sorry," he said, frustrated more by his lack of control than by Charles's comment.

"I haven't," Charles said gently. "I'm just saying that the question needs to be examined."

"Fine. I'll examine it. Jeremiah owed Breckenridge two million dollars. Which just happened to be the ransom amount. And that's a coincidence I'm not prepared to ignore." He looked at Jackson.

"Guess we're going to San Diego," Jackson said, then grinned. "Gotta love these family reunions."

"Family reunion?"

Damien turned at the sound of Nikki's voice, then dropped to his knees and held out his arms for the two little girls barreling toward him with cries of "Daddy! Daddy!"

"Hey, pumpkins!" He brushed kisses over their foreheads, then stood up, Lara latched to his back like a monkey and Anne clinging to his leg. He looked at Nikki and saw the smile reach all the way to her eyes. And for that moment—one brilliant, glorious moment—all was right with the world.

Reality crashed back with Lara's question. "Are we having a party, Daddy? There's lotsa people here."

"Unca Jackson!" Anne squealed, releasing Damien to run to her uncle.

"Hey, sweetstuff," Jackson said, pulling Anne into his lap as he answered Lara. "Not a party, baby girl. Just some work stuff."

Damien couldn't see Lara's face since she was clinging to his back, but he could tell by the room's reaction that she'd displayed one of her famous eye rolls as she'd announced, "That's boring!"

"I'm guessing this isn't the kind of family reunion you were talking about," Nikki said, coming to take Lara off his back as she nodded toward Jackson, who was occupied with Anne, and Sylvia, who'd just come in from the back rooms to join her husband.

"Jackson and I are heading to San Diego tomorrow," he told both women. Considering the shadows that crossed their faces, he was certain they both knew exactly what that meant.

"You think he's involved," Nikki said.

"I think he might be."

"Makes sense," Jamie said, curling her small body onto Ryan's lap and hooking an arm around his neck. Her long hair was pulled back in a ponytail, and now she tugged the band free, sending dark waves tumbling over his shoulder.

"Who?" Bree asked, looking around at everyone as she stepped into the room.

"Let's let the girls finish saying goodnight and get them to bed," Nikki said. "I'll tell you on the way."

"Sure—I just..." She trailed off, looking between Damien and Ryan. "I only ... well, what I mean is, he's really dead? Rory? And you really think he was working with someone else?"

"He is," Damien said. "And we do."

"I want to help," she said earnestly. "I know the target was Anne, but he took me too. And if Rory was working with someone, then that someone dragged me into this. I want to help figure out who. You'll let me, right?" She turned, laying eyes on everyone in the room before stopping at Damien. "You have to let me. If someone had used you this way—"

"Yes," he said, working to keep his voice level. "Of course you can help."

She nodded, satisfied, but Damien was anything but. He glanced at Nikki and saw the same grief reflected on her face. Bree was so damn innocent, or she had been. She was starting college soon. Off to a big adventure. This wasn't the kind of baggage she was supposed to have when she set out on that journey. She should have no cares other than paying tuition, studying for finals, and debating what to wear for her date Friday night. But she'd moved into his world, and now she was begging to chase monsters.

It was like he was a magnet for pain and suffering.

No.

Brutally, he shoved the dark thoughts away. He was tired—no, he was beyond tired. But he hadn't caused this. Hadn't dragged Bree down into the abyss. That was on Rory's shoulders. Rory, and some unknown puppet master.

or really early or something?"

"That would be terrific." Lara and Anne both adored Ryan's younger sister, and he knew that her school schedule was light.

"Will do. And I'll think about who else I can talk to."

"We should have his mobile and computer soon. Paper address book if he has one. Charles is pulling some strings," Quincy added, in response to Damien's questioning glance.

"Okay," Bree said. "I can go through it. Maybe I'll remember some offhand comment and it'll blow the case wide open. That happens, right? It always happens in the movies."

"I'm sure it'll happen just like that," Damien said, then laughed when she rolled her eyes.

"I'm going to go peek in on the girls," she said before hurrying away.

"You did good with her." Damien nodded to Quincy as he stood, stretching. "Not likely to be dangerous, but something that lets her really feel like she's helping. And might actually produce a solid lead."

"We had to rely on civilians a lot at Deliverance. After all, we were flying under the radar."

"And British Intelligence?"

"Ah, that's a horse of a different color. The motto there is to avoid all civilian interference. I lead a double life, my friend. Or I did. It's all a bit up in the air now that Deliverance is winding down."

"I wanted to talk to you about that." He sat again, this time perched on the edge of the table, one foot on the seat of his chair. "I know Ryan's mentioned it to you, but I want to reiterate how much we both hope you'll come on board at Stark International. And I want to assure you I can make it worth your while. Both financially and with the work you'd be doing. No holing up in a warehouse for days doing surveillance, I promise."

Quincy laughed. "I'm flattered. And I'm intrigued by what you and Ryan are planning. A specialty team inside your corporate security group."

"Something that flies under the radar," Damien said, encouraged by Quincy's response. "Lately, I've been thinking more and more about people who don't have my resources, and I wonder how they survive the uncertainty. Hell, I can barely survive. It would be a for-profit entity with a significant pro bono presence."

"Like one of your foundations, only for chasing down bad guys instead of educating kids."

"Not a bad way to put it."

"Like I said, it's a great idea, and I'm chuffed you thought of me. But the truth is, I'm thinking of retiring."

Damien studied him, nodding slowly. "Mind if I ask why?" He hadn't known Quincy long, but he'd seen the man in action. And he didn't seem like the type to retire so young. Not when there was work yet to be done.

For a moment, Quincy didn't answer. Then he said simply, "Secrets." A moment passed, then another. Then he lifted a shoulder, shrugging. "And lies. That about sums up this business."

"MI6 or Deliverance?"

"Ah, I can't tell you that, my friend. Reference the aforementioned secrets."

Damien chuckled. "Fair enough."

"I'll say this though about Deliverance—we had more successes than failures, but even then, that life takes a toll. I got into it because of Dallas. I was there the night he was kidnapped, you know. I'd followed him. I saw it happen. And I'd been completely fucking helpless. So I shared his obsession. That driving need to find his kidnapper. To make it right for him and Jane."

He drew a breath. "But he has his answers now—and a wife who loves him. He's made the decision to get out, and I think it's the right one. God knows he served his time. But, Damien, I think I have, too."

"You're good," Damien said, because as far as he was concerned, there was no greater praise than competence.

"I am. But—" He turned away, his expression suddenly guarded.

"Quince?"

"I'm good," he repeated, turning back with the flash of a quick smile. "And I'm in this with you for now. But the future's a long way off, Stark. We don't need to worry about that right now."

Damien knew better than to press. There were other ways to find out about the shadows behind Quincy's eyes. "Fair enough. And again, I'm very glad you're here."

He slid off the table, intending to go see his daughters before checking in with Ryan. But he hesitated, then turned back to Quincy. "You worked with Dallas. You witnessed his kidnapping."

Quincy tilted his head, waiting for Damien to continue.

"If the worst happens," Damien began, hating to even voice the question but knowing he had to. "If we never find the bastard—how do I live without knowing who did this?" The words burned in his throat, thick and bitter. "Never facing the man who took my daughter? Who tormented my nanny, my friend? How do I live, knowing he's still out there? Still drawing breath?"

Quincy's shoulders sagged, and he rose from his chair. "Honestly, I don't know." He reached out, pressing his hand down on Damien's shoulder. "But I'm going to work my ass off so that hopefully you won't have to find out."

* * * *

Quincy's words hung over Damien as he knelt at the side of Anne's toddler bed, watching her chest rise and fall, her cupid bow lips parted, her innocent little face free of marks of fear or lines of regret. She had her whole life ahead of her, but that future could have been so easily ripped away. And every time he recalled that simple truth, a wild and dangerous fury ripped through him.

Like Quincy, Damien was going to work his ass off to find the kidnapper. Spend whatever it took, bribe whoever demanded it. Cut whatever corners needed cutting.

Whatever it took, he would make it happen. And in the end, he'd find the man. Then he'd stare into the bastard's eyes. And he would fucking end this.

He'd do that because he had to. Because otherwise there would come a day when Anne knew the truth about the horror lurking out in the world. And once she knew, that face would no longer be filled with innocent trust. Fear would lurk under the surface, tainting everything. And when he looked into her eyes, he would surely see recrimination looking back.

"I'm so sorry, angel," he whispered, then bent to kiss her, breathing in that clean baby scent—Ivory soap, Johnson's baby shampoo, and a hint of powder.

She yawned, her fingers clutching the striped hospital blanket that had been her lovey from the day she'd come home. Stuffed animals held no interest for her, but she'd throw the tantrum of the century if she went to sleep without that lovey.

Another bolt of anger shot through him as he realized she hadn't had the blanket in the days she'd been gone. He'd taken her. He'd drugged her, supposedly to make the ordeal easier to bear. And yet he'd offered her no real comfort at all.

Death offered Rory no comfort either, as Damien was sure he was rotting in hell.

And soon, the puppet master would join him. Somehow, some way, Damien would make sure of that.

That question he'd asked Quincy? A question about how he could handle the weight of failure? Not a problem. He wouldn't fail. They'd fucked with the wrong man, and Damien was going to destroy them.

One way or another, if he had to spend every dime to his name, he would find the bastard, and he would make him pay.

Chapter Seventeen

When he didn't find Nikki in their bedroom, he went back to the open area. Charles had already gone home, and Quincy and Jackson were packing up. "Syl's already in the car," Jackson said. "She wanted to call the kids before bedtime. Where are we meeting in the morning?"

"Meet me at my private hangar at the Santa Monica airport. I'll fly us down in the Cessna."

"Nine?"

"Perfect."

Jackson started to walk away, then paused. He turned back, and Damien saw his own determination reflected back in the icy blue of his brother's eyes.

"We'll find out if Jeremiah is behind this," Jackson said. "And if he is, he'll pay."

Damien gave him a nod of acknowledgement that was insufficient to show how much he appreciated Jackson's support. *Everyone's* support, he amended, responding to Quincy's wave goodnight, then finding Ryan still working hard on a laptop.

"Get some rest. Then come back fresh tomorrow with the rest of the team."

"That was my plan," Ryan said. "But Jamie got commandeered by Ollie and your wife." He nodded toward the balcony, and Damien saw the moonlit forms of the three friends beyond the glass.

"I'm glad they carved out some time despite this day going off the rails."

Ryan shot him a wry grin. "Understatement much?"

"I'm going to go tell Ollie and Jamie goodnight. And catch you after San Diego."

Ryan's expression sobered. "I don't envy you the trip."

"Funny, I can't wait to look into that man's eyes. And I'll know the truth. He's a liar and a son-of-a-bitch, but I know him. And if he's behind this, I'll see it." He met Ryan's gaze. "And then it'll be your job to prove it."

"I hate that you have a father who falls under the umbrella of likely suspects."

Damien waved the comment away. He held no illusions about his father. And, he thought as he crossed the room, he'd gotten over feeling sorry for himself about his paternity long ago.

When he reached the balcony, Ollie turned in surprise, and Damien realized that he was the only one there.

"Oh, hey," Ollie said. "You just missed the girls. They went down to the pool deck. Guess they wanted to run to the guest house and tell Bree something."

"No problem. I'll let Ryan know." He started to go back inside, but paused when Ollie asked him to hang on a second.

Damien turned back, then leaned against the rail and waited.

"Right," Ollie said, clearing his throat. "I, you know, just wanted to say thanks for letting me stay and help."

"On the contrary. I'm grateful to have your insight."

"Cool." He slid his hands into his pockets. "And, I wanted to say thanks for not holding a grudge about the whole money thing."

Months ago, Ollie had privately asked Damien to help him out financially so that he wouldn't lose an investment property he'd bought in the hills. After reviewing the plans and financials, Damien had declined. "You were in over your head. At that point you were better off walking. At least, that's what I believed based on the paperwork you gave me to review." He looked pointedly at Ollie. Ollie looked away.

"Care to give me the full story now?" After the recent revelation that Ollie was now working with the FBI, Damien had realized that Ollie's request for help had been part of some sort of investigation.

"Wish I could. Just trust me when I say that you were only being looked at because you fit a profile. I told them there was no way you were involved."

Damien raised a brow. "That's a new tune from you, McKee."

"No." Ollie shook his head as if to underscore the word. "Look, I know we've had our moments. And when you first got with Nikki I tried to warn her off. But you have a code, Stark. Maybe it took me awhile to see it, but there are lines you don't cross, and one of them is skirting the law where your business is concerned. Won't happen." He shrugged as if in apology. "I probably stayed in the 'Stark's an A-Hole' camp for longer than I should have, but I had reason. Nikki's special to me."

"I know." For that matter, Damien was pretty certain he understood that better than Ollie did. After all, Damien knew full well that Ollie was in love with his wife. But as far as Damien could tell, Ollie hadn't admitted that to himself. And, unfortunately, he was certain that until Ollie admitted it and let her go, he'd never manage to maintain a relationship.

"What was the scam?" Damien deliberately changed the subject.

"All I can say is that there's a major financial racket going on in the world of renovation and house flipping. And that nobody thinks you're involved. Plus, since you are in the clear, I can tell you that I really do own the property, I really am planning on renovating, and I'm having no trouble making my payments."

"Fair enough. I'm going to go find Nikki. And Ollie, I mean it. It's good that you're here."

"One more thing—the vandalism at Nikki's office. I know it's not the priority here, but I was talking to Quincy and Ryan, and I may have access to some security footage that the guys have been trying to locate."

"That would be great."

"I'll let you know. Whoever would do something like that to Nikki... That guy's a fucking worm."

Damien nodded. He and Ollie might never really be friends. But their love for Nikki? *That* was their bond.

* * * *

In the end, Damien didn't find Nikki until he returned to the master bedroom, saw the flicker of candlelight coming from the attached bathroom, and found his naked wife sipping a glass of Pinot Noir in the massive, bubble-filled whirlpool tub. The flames of dozens of tiny tea lights flickered around her, making her skin and hair glow.

For a moment, he simply stood there, lost in her beauty. In the way she leaned back, her eyes closed, her breasts barely visible above the bubbles. And when she lifted a bath sponge and let it drip on her neck, his balls tightened and his cock turned to steel.

He wanted to touch her. To taste her. And then, when she lifted her hands out of the water and stroked her breasts, he knew that what he wanted to do most of all was watch her. The way her lips parted as she rolled her nipples between two fingers. The way her body arched as she kept one hand on her breast, but slid the other slowly down her body.

Her eyes were closed, and he heard her breathing come quicker. The gasps as her hand found that sensitive spot he knew so well. Her body moved—just small motions, but enough to make the water dance around her and the bubbles sparkle in the candlelight.

He imagined the slick feel of her on his fingertips. The tight nub of her clit. The tight, slick heat of her core.

"*Damien.*"

His heart skipped, and he watched her face, then realized that she didn't realize he was there. She was calling to him only in her fantasy. And damned if he didn't almost come right then.

Her breathing quickened, and he stepped closer, moving to the end of the tub so that he could see her face. The way her skin flushed with arousal. Her breasts, dappled with soap bubbles, her hard nipples peeking out, begging him to suck on them. Her knees rested on either side of the tub, and though the bubbles had started out dense, some were melting, and he could see the movement of her hand as she stroked herself, her hips moving as one hand teased her clit.

As he watched, she bit her lower lip, then closed her free hand over her breast. She stroked it, caressing her nipple lightly, then tugging at it to a point that was surely painful. She bucked, making the water slosh out of the tub, and her soft moans echoed in the large bathroom.

He realized with surprise that he was stroking himself through his pants, and that he was close. Possibly as close as she was. He closed his eyes, striving to regain some control, and when he opened them again, he found her looking right back at him.

"Do you want me?" His voice was raw. Rough.

"Always," she said. "But no." She licked her lips, then looked away as if shy. "I want you to watch."

"Christ, Nikki."

She tilted her head so that she was facing him again. For a moment, she held his gaze, her hand beneath the water stroking in slow, rhythmic motions. "Come on, baby," he urged, but she just shook her head. And instead of continuing to play with her clit, she slid two fingers deep inside, arching her head back and lifting her hips as she finger-fucked herself, slow and deep, then faster as her arousal spiked.

She met his eyes, then drew her hand free, her fingers once again on her clit as she rubbed tight circles, then closed her eyes, her body tense. His, too. Then she gasped, her body shaking as she made the sounds he heard so often in bed. Sounds designed to make him hard. To make his blood heat.

Sounds that pushed him to the edge.

And oh, fuck, he was close right now.

"Please," she said. "Oh, yes, oh, please." Then she bucked up, splashing what seemed like gallons of water onto the tile floors. And as she exploded, there was only one word on her lips—"Damien."

He lost it.

He absolutely fucking lost it. He hadn't intended to come, not like that. But dear God, what she did to him.

He stood there, still fully clothed, a goddamn satisfied mess, as he watched his very smug wife extend a hand to him.

"I think it's only right I help you clean up."

"You think so?"

A slow, sexy grin eased across her face. "I may have other things in mind, too. Guess we'll have to see. Right now, I need you naked."

"Never let it be said I failed to give my wife exactly what she needed."

She started to reply, but he pressed a finger over his lips, silencing her. He unbuttoned his shirt, slipped out of it, then dropped it on the floor. He'd already taken his shoes and socks off in the bedroom, and now he stripped out of the pants and briefs. Naked, he moved into the warm water to sit in front of her, lifting her extended legs onto his so that their bodies crossed.

Silently, he cupped her waist, then moved her within easy kissing distance. And because kisses were on his mind, he did just that, holding her by the neck as he bent forward until his mouth was on hers. Sweetly gentle at first. A tiny taste. A delicious lick. Their mouths played softly, their breathing came harder, and their small sounds of pleasure floated around them, buoying them up.

Soon, though, passion increased, and those nips and teases grew into slow, heated kisses. The kind that made a woman wet. That made a man go hard.

One hand was behind her head and he slid it around, trailing kisses down her arched neck as his fingertips followed the path to her breast. He teased her nipple, rolling it hard between his thumb and forefinger. Then bent to close his mouth over her other breast, tasting skin and soap and the heady flavor of his wife. This incredible woman who quelled his demons and stilled his ever-churning thoughts.

And he didn't want to think. Didn't want the day circulating in his head. Not now.

Instead, he wanted the respite that only Nikki could bring.

She slid her hands up his thighs until she reached his cock, then stroked him with her bath-oiled fingers. He felt himself go harder, that wild need to bring her closer—to claim her so intimately they became one—burning through him. Moving his hands to her hips, he slid his fingers between her legs, thrusting slowly in and out as she rocked her hips, taking him deeper, and with each thrust, teasing her clit on the pad of his thumb.

"Is that what you want, baby? You want to come again, you greedy girl?"

"Oh, God, yes," she said, the fervency of her response making his cock ache.

This was what he needed. This moment, this woman. A reprieve from the noise and the drama and the horror, lost here in the arms of his wife, his love. A few moments to feel as though all was right with the world. And to let himself believe that between the two of them, they had the power to keep the nightmares away, even if only for a little bit.

She trembled in his arms, so full of erotic electricity he was surprised that sparks weren't shooting across the tub, burning them to cinders. She was close, ready to explode, and he wanted—hell, *needed*—to feel her body tighten around him when she did.

He slid closer until he was almost in the middle of the tub, then met her eyes as he ordered, "On me, baby. I want you to ride my cock."

He saw the heat flare in her eyes as her teeth dragged over her lower lip.

"I like the way that sounds," she said, her voice husky with desire. She shifted in the tub, and he held her perfect ass as one of her hands rested on his shoulders. The other slipped under the water to find his shaft, then slowly stroked, managing—because she was a goddamn miracle worker—to make him even harder.

"Don't tease me, Nikki. I want to feel your cunt, hot and wet, around me."

She moaned, just as he knew she would. He loved how responsive she was. How turned on she got when he talked dirty, telling her exactly what he wanted, what he planned.

"That's it," he said as she guided him to her core, and he felt her exquisite tight heat as she lowered herself, taking him all the way inside her. "Oh, baby, that's perfect. Tell me what you want."

"Kiss me," she said, her hips moving in a slow, sensual rhythm, warm water splashing around them.

His cock twitched inside her, just from the heated desire in her voice. He used one hand to cup her head as he claimed her mouth, relishing the taste of her. The way her fingers threaded through his hair, urging him closer, as if nothing else in the world mattered except the pleasure of their connection.

At first, her hips were still and the kiss deep but gentle. But he needed more, *craved* more, and he drew her tighter against him, his tongue no longer exploring, but demanding. She matched him thrust for thrust, their tongues warring, their lips teasing, their teeth clashing.

She had both hands on his head as she held him close, her mouth a frenzy against his, her fingers tight in his hair, so that the only way he could leave her embrace would be to literally rip himself free. But he never wanted to leave. Right then, he wanted this moment to last forever.

His hand found her breast, and he stroked her smooth skin. She bit his lip, then arched back in pleasure when he pinched her nipple, her cry of, "Yes, God yes," reverberating through him.

He took advantage of her new position by lowering his mouth, this time teasing her nipple with his teeth, biting then sucking then biting again. She tasted as incredible as she felt, and her moans and cries sent them both spiraling higher, spinning closer to release. To that wild moment when pleasure overcomes the pain of utter destruction. Because she would destroy him. How many times had he exploded in her arms? *La petite mort*. The little death. And oh, how he longed for it now.

Her hips rocked faster as she rode him, wild and hot, the motion making waves in the tub, sending water splashing over the sides. Forget slow and sensual. This was a hard, wild fuck, and dear God he loved it. Loved *her*.

"Play with your clit, baby," he ordered, his voice low.

She met his eyes. "You do it for me."

"Oh, no," he said, then kissed her hard as he slid his hand, now slick with bath oil, down her back. Lower and lower until his fingertip found her ass and teased the tight little muscle. She gasped, then bit her lower lip. He waited, just in case she wanted to protest, but she just rocked slowly against him as she lifted her hands to tease her own breasts.

"Baby," he murmured, easing his finger inside and watching her eyes go dark with passion.

"Touch yourself," he repeated, his free hand behind him to keep them steady. "My finger's otherwise occupied."

She didn't answer aloud, but she slid one hand down from her breast to disappear under the water. Then he felt the brush of her fingers against his cock as she teased her clit while riding him, her motions coming faster and faster as her climax bore down on her. When she finally came, the explosion was so intense that the clenching of her muscles around his finger and his cock drove him over the edge, too.

His body shattered, and he grabbed one of her hips, desperate for the leverage to thrust her down, deeper and harder, craving that last intense connection before his entire body went limp, sated and satisfied.

She fell forward on top of him, breathing hard and practically buzzing with pleasure. He wrapped his arms around her, then simply clung to her, as the water cooled around them.

"I love you," he whispered. And though there was more he could tell her—enough words to fill an eternity—right then, those three words were enough.

Chapter Eighteen

Damien brought the Cessna in for the final approach. Below him, the runway stretched out. A long, straight path, and all he had to do was follow it home.

Straightforward. Simple. And in a few moments, he and Jackson would be in San Diego on the ground safe and sound. Because all that was required for that outcome was that he not fuck up the landing.

Wasn't that a mirror of life? Love, a family, children. He'd fought for what he had, for the family he'd built. And yet somehow, he'd been knocked off the path.

Somehow, he'd fucked up.

He just didn't know how or where, and right now, it felt as though he was standing too close to a Monet, the dabs of colored brushstrokes not making sense. But if he could step back and look at it from a different perspective, then the entire picture would become clear.

Maybe it would be clear when he stood back and looked at his father.

"You're expecting it to be him," Jackson said once they were on the road.

"Aren't you?"

Jackson drew in a breath, then turned and looked out the window as Damien maneuvered the rented Lexus toward the hilltop home their father had bought a few years ago. For a moment, Jackson said nothing, and Damien started to think his brother wasn't going to answer. Then Jackson spoke, the words measured and low.

"He's not a good man," Jackson said. "And the more I learn of him, the more I know that I won't change my mind about that. I think of myself as a good man, but sometimes I wonder if I'm just delusional. Because how can I have come from Jeremiah Stark and have the slightest bit of good in me?"

Damien clutched the steering wheel as Jackson voiced what he'd felt his whole life. Hell, what he'd been fighting his whole life. "Neither one of us is our father," he said, as much to himself as to Jackson. "And I can testify that you are a good man. And that means a lot coming from a man who thought you were a conniving prick the first time we met."

As he'd hoped, Jackson chuckled, then turned to face Damien. "Fair enough. But here's the thing—as vile as I think our father is—and even knowing something about what he allowed Richter to do to you—I can't imagine him putting Anne at risk. Can you? Can you really?"

Damien stiffened, those dark days filling his mind. All the times he'd begged his father to let him off the circuit. The moment he realized his father knew exactly what was going on.

"Why? Why can't we just hire a new coach?"

"It's not that simple."

A wild fury ripped through Damien. "Simple?" His voice broke and he hated himself for it. "Do you know what he does to me? What he—never mind. Forget it. Never mind."

"I know what he can do. And that's take you all the way to the top and make us one hell of a lot of money in the process. Seems to me that whatever he wants—all this noise that you're sniveling about—is a small price to pay for fame and for fortune."

In the Lexus, Damien suppressed a shiver. "I can," he said. "I don't have any problems imagining it at all."

* * * *

"This is why my sons visit me?" Jeremiah Stark paced the sunlit living room like a wildcat. He came to a stop in front of Jackson, then turned angry eyes on Damien.

They'd laid the whole story on him. Rory's murder. The logical conclusion suggested by Jeremiah's two million dollar debt. And then Damien had told him what he believed.

"You really think that's possible?" Jeremiah focused on Damien's face. "You really believe that I could have had something to do with that sweet baby girl being yanked away from you?"

"Yeah," Damien said evenly. "I do."

"Well, fuck you, Mister Big Shot." Jeremiah's voice shook but he stood his ground. "Fuck you," he repeated, then punctuated the words by slamming his palm unexpectedly against Damien's chest, sending his body stumbling backwards and his fury spiraling up.

"Okay, whoa there." Jackson said as Damien righted himself and surged forward. "Both of you, just retreat to your corners."

"Did you hear him?" Jeremiah said. "Were you listening to what he's accusing me of?"

"Not an accusation. Not yet. But we're looking at a two million dollar ransom when you're staring down a two million dollar debt. That deserves a question. And that's why we're here. To ask the question."

"Well, you have your answer. So get the hell out of my house."

"Your house," Damien said slowly. "And how exactly did you earn the money to buy this house?"

Jeremiah said nothing, just stared defiantly at the wall.

"You've lived off me for most of my life, and I put up with it despite the hell you put me through. It was easier to write you a check than to listen to your begging and excuses and lame justifications. I paid you off to keep you away, Jeremiah. But then I shut off the flow. And I just know that pissed you off."

"I didn't—"

Damien held up a hand, cutting him off. "I know you were pissed, *Dad*. How could you not be? Your steady income suddenly all dried up. And now there's debt and no way for you to pay it off."

He took a step toward his father, his body tense, ready to lash out. *Wanting* to lash out. "Is that why you did it? To get money for the debt?" His voice rose with his anger. "Or was it more than that? Were you punishing me for cutting you out? Cutting you off?"

He felt Jackson's hand on his shoulder and realized that he'd inched so close that his father was pressed up against the closed glass door, and Damien was only millimeters from his face. "Back it off, brother."

With a violent jerk, Damien shrugged out from Jackson's touch and turned away, furious with himself for coming so close to snapping.

He took a deep breath, then another.

"I didn't—"

"*No.*" The word was hard and firm, and as he spoke it, Damien turned back around, not driven by fury this time, but by a rage that burned colder. Deeper. "I don't want to hear your excuses. I don't want to hear your denials. I just want to tell you this—if I find out that you had anything to do with my daughter's kidnapping, then you're a dead man. Plain and simple."

"I didn't." Jeremiah's voice broke. "Christ, son—"

"Do *not* call me that."

"Damien. Damien, please. You have to believe me. I have no idea who took Anne. I didn't know Rory was dead until you told me. And other than your money, I don't have a clue as to why anyone would want to take her."

"I want to believe you," Damien admitted. "God knows why, because it would damn sure be easier if you confessed right now and we just fucking ended this. But I want to believe you." He shot a glance toward Jackson. "Maybe I just want to believe that the blood that flows in my veins isn't completely reprehensible. But it's hard, old man. Because I've spent a lifetime learning what you're capable of. So don't you dare tell me that you could never do that to my little girl. Because I know better. Believe me, Jeremiah. I know the truth because I've seen the darkness."

"But I *wouldn't.*" Though there were no tears, Jeremiah's words were practically a sob. "Don't you get it? Those baby girls are my redemption. I can't soil that. I can't screw it up."

Damien glanced at Jackson, saw that his brother looked as confused as he felt.

"You," Jeremiah said, pointing at Jackson. "God knows I wasn't a decent father to you. And as for you—do you think I don't know how much I messed up? How much I messed you up? And God, even Sofia. I actually went and added that poor girl to the mix. That's how low I sunk. I fucked up, Damien. I know that. I *know* it. But not those little girls," he said fiercely. "Never those little girls. They're redemption. Yours and mine. And that's a chance I won't fuck up."

"Redemption." Damien stared at him, the word hovering over his head like a storm cloud. "*Redemption?*" He took a single step toward Jeremiah, then stopped, afraid if he got too close he'd be unable to resist the temptation to lash out and bloody the man. "My children are not your way into my good graces. And just so we're clear, there is nothing—*nothing*—you can do to redeem yourself."

Jeremiah swallowed, his eyes cast down. "Maybe that's true," he said, his voice so low it was barely audible. "But I didn't have anything to do with Anne's kidnapping. I didn't hurt her, Damien. And I swear to you, I never will."

Chapter Nineteen

When Damien walked back into the Malibu house at just after five, the place was bustling.

He'd parted ways with Jackson at the airport with a promise to call if the team learned anything. In the meantime, Jackson would once again be taking point on The Domino while Damien carved out time to pursue the Rory investigation.

"Give yourself a limit," Jackson had told him. "You're not an investigator, and you have a business to run. One week in the thick of it, and if you don't have answers by then, you back off and let Ryan's people do their thing."

It was good advice, but that didn't mean he would follow it. Right now, he couldn't think past the next step.

Unfortunately, he didn't know what the next step was.

He reluctantly believed Jeremiah. Not so much because he believed the older man had warm, fuzzy feelings for his grandchildren, but because he didn't think Jeremiah had the balls to pull off a kidnapping, much less risk the fallout if he was caught. Jeremiah Stark was not a man who would do well in prison, and he had to know that.

And Jackson was right about Breckenridge. He'd boldly asked to be invited back into The Domino. Which meant he was either innocent or the boldest motherfucker on the planet.

With a frustrated sigh, he stepped off the stairs and into the chaos, then was rewarded when Nikki slid into his arms, a glass of Scotch in her hand for him. "The gatehouse guard called to let me know you were back. I thought you could use this."

He grinned, the weight of the day sliding away from nothing more than the feel of the woman in his arms. "You have no idea," he said, accepting the glass and giving her a very thorough kiss before taking a long, life-sustaining swallow.

Across the room, he saw Evelyn standing with Frank. He glanced down at Nikki, who nodded. "I think they've smoothed things over," she said, drawing him toward the small seating area at the top of the stairs.

She pulled him down onto the love seat, then sat next to him, one leg tucked under her so that she was looking at him as she continued. "I still don't know exactly what's between them, but I think he's gained back whatever points Evelyn docked him when he didn't come home for me right away."

"He's trying to be a good father," Damien said. "I respect that. It's not an easy job."

"You make it look easy."

The words, so simple, shot straight to his heart. "I love you," he said. "And God knows I'm trying."

She leaned closer and kissed him. "Do you want to talk about today with Jeremiah?"

He made a scoffing noise. "It's a rare day when I actually want to talk about Jeremiah. But, dammit, Nikki, he—" He cut himself off, a red-hot flare of anger making him grind his teeth and shake his head.

"Damien?" He heard an edge of panic in her voice. "Wait, wait a second. Are you saying—I mean, is he really involved? What did he say? Why would you wait so long to tell me?"

"No. Baby, no." He stroked her arm. "I'm sorry I scared you. I thought it was him, but it's not."

"Then, what?"

The fury he'd tamped down began to boil. "Redemption," he said, anger driving him to his feet. "My father said the girls were his redemption. And mine. *Bastard.*"

He saw a reflection of his own pain in her eyes. Then she stood, too. She slid one arm around his waist, her other hand going to cup his head as she lifted herself up on her toes and kissed him. Gently at first, but then he drew her in closer, claiming her mouth, taking what he needed. And, dammit, he did need it. Needed *her.* Her support surrounding him, and her love filling him.

"Redemption," he murmured as they pulled apart. "*You're* my redemption."

She smiled, but it was bittersweet. "You're wrong, you know. We're a lot of things to each other, Damien, but I'm not your redemption. Because you don't need redemption. You're a good man, and you always have been."

He looked at her face and saw that she believed those words. "Thank you," he said, even though he knew damn well that they weren't true.

* * * *

The hum and buzz of electronics and conversation filled the third floor, so much so that Damien almost didn't hear the house phone. He snatched the handset up from the credenza, then frowned when the guard on duty announced the waiting guest.

"Nikki?" He lifted a hand to catch her attention, and she looked up from where she was reviewing the transcript of Rory's confession and the formal statement he'd made when entering his plea. A long shot, but maybe he'd said something useful. "Did you order food?"

Her brow furrowed in confusion, and he was about to tell the guard to hold the scammer—probably a reporter trying to gain access—when Bree bounced across the room. "That was me. It's Kari. She's bringing by all the breads and cookies and pastries and stuff that were left over today."

He must have looked baffled, because she went on. "I thought everyone could use the pick-me-up. That's okay, right?"

"Very okay," he said. "And very thoughtful. You can let her through," he added to the guard, who still lingered on the line.

"I'll go meet her at the door," Bree said.

As she hurried down the stairs, he heard Ryan calling him over.

"What have you got?"

"Just come. You need to see this." Ryan's voice was low and level. "You, too, Nikki."

"Something concrete?" He moved across the floor, coming to a stop behind the end of the table where Ryan had set up his laptop. He held out his left hand to Nikki, who had risen from her chair and come to stand behind him.

"Is it a lead on whoever was manipulating Rory?" she asked,

twining her fingers with his own.

"Not Rory," Ryan said. "Nikki's office. Hang on, I've just about got this." Ryan fiddled with a control panel that he'd plugged into one of his computer ports. Immediately, the third-floor projection screen descended and all windows that lit the room were shuttered, blocking out the waning light from the descending sun.

A moment later, as he heard the front door open and Bree chattering with Kari, the screen glowed white, then with a test pattern, then white again. Soon, grainy video footage started to play, a timecode running along the bottom.

"Is that—"

"The alley that runs behind your office building," Damien confirmed for her.

"But I thought—" Nikki began.

"So did I," Damien said, frowning at Ryan. "I thought there were no functional cameras back there." They'd hoped that the perp had driven to the office and had parked in the small pay-for-parking lot two buildings down from Nikki's office. Unfortunately, the security cameras for that lot had been tampered with a week before the vandalism occurred, and the lot owner hadn't yet fixed them. The few other businesses that had cameras only aimed them at their own back doors.

And yet here was broad, high definition video coverage of the entire parking lot and a significant chunk of the alley leading all the way to the intersection. If Nikki's vandal parked in that lot—or even just walked down the alley—they'd see.

"I don't understand," Nikki said. "Without cameras, where did this come from?"

Ryan tilted his head to indicate Ollie, who was coming to stand on the other side of Ryan's workstation.

"What? How?" Nikki asked, voicing Damien's thoughts.

Ollie shrugged nonchalantly, as if the whole thing was no big deal. But Damien saw the pride on his face, and knew that Ollie was pleased to be able to help. "Long story, but the bottom line is that the FBI has had a surveillance camera on that parking lot for a while. Nothing the FBI is interested in happened on that night, so I was able to get the footage copied for you."

"And *we* are definitely interested," Ryan said. "From my preliminary scan, I think we may have caught the perp on video."

"Ollie!" Nikki ran to him and gave him a hug. "That's amazing."

"It really is," Damien said, following Nikki and shaking Ollie's hand.

"Perhaps we should hold off on showering him with praise until we see if the clarity is sufficient for an ID," Quincy said, coming over from the far end of the table, where he'd been giving instructions to one of Ryan's techies, an eager young man who looked to be scrolling through data at the speed of light.

"Okay, here goes." Ryan started to manipulate the video, fast-forwarding until a person entered the frame. "There, see? Look at this." The screen split into two columns, the new video on the left and the security video from Nikki's office on the right. On the right, they saw the now-familiar tall, thin figure in a white hoodie carrying a shopping bag.

"That's our vandal," Damien said.

"Bags look to be holding spray paint cans, and the timing is right," Ryan agreed. "So, yeah, that's the assumption."

"Now we're looking for him on the other footage?" Nikki asked. "Hoping that we'll see his face so that we can ID him?"

"That's the plan," Ollie confirmed. "He probably kept his head down in the building on purpose. But he might not be so guarded outside."

"Enhance the image," Quincy said, and Ryan nodded as he manipulated the mouse, zooming in on the video footage of the alley until they were tight on the person walking across the screen, same outfit, the hood up, their head down.

"That's not a guy," Nikki said, her hands on the table as she leaned toward the screen. She turned to look at Damien, then Ryan. "See how she's moving? Her hips."

"Are you sure?" Ollie asked.

She turned to him. "Have you met my mother? I spent most of elementary and high school studying video tapes of women walking."

"You may be right," Quincy said. "But it's all bloody useless unless we get a face. Boy, girl, teen, adult. We need more to go on."

"Hell," Damien said. "This isn't going to—oh, fuck." The word was ripped out of him, torn out by the image on the screen. Tall and thin, with a face he knew well.

Nikki was right. Their vandal was woman.

"Sofia?"

Nikki whispered the word, her voice full of pain. Damien ripped his attention away from the horrific image on the screen to find Nikki looking back at him, her haunted eyes breaking his heart. He took a step forward, as much to soothe as to be soothed, but she backed away, her hand up as if to ward him off.

"Nikki—"

"No." She licked her lips, her eyes darting around the room. "Just, no." For a moment she stood frozen, then she released a shaky breath. "You told me we could trust her," she whispered. "That she was better. You promised me that, and then she went and destroyed my office? Called me a bitch?"

The words, so horrible and true, sliced his heart wide open. He wanted to scream an apology. To beg her forgiveness.

But he just stood there, shattering under the force of his failure, as she turned and hurried away.

Chapter Twenty

It might have been an eternity, or perhaps it was only an instant. Damien didn't know. All he knew was that he'd stood there, useless, as Nikki left, leaving her tattered trust behind.

On his other side, Quincy bit out a curse. Damien barely heard it. He knew he needed to go to Nikki—needed to hold his wife in his arms and let her cry and grieve. He knew that—but goddamn it, how the hell could he do it, knowing that he was the one who had caused her pain? That she'd run from him when she was hurting, instead of into his arms.

"I need to check on her." He said the words to no one in particular, then started toward the master bedroom, assuming that's where she'd gone. He didn't make it, though. He was brought to a stop by the quick, firm tug on the back of his shirt.

He turned to find Jamie shaking her head. "Let her go, okay? Just give her a few minutes to let it all settle. Seriously, D. It'll be okay. But that bitch has been a thorn in her side from the beginning."

"That's why I need—"

"No. You don't."

"Goddammit, Jamie. You can't—"

"She's right." Ryan's voice was soft but firm. "She's not saying forever, she's just saying for now. Give Nikki some time to figure out how she even feels."

He looked around the room, one of the few times he'd ever felt helpless. And he damn sure didn't like the feeling. "Well?" he demanded, when Evelyn came over, his pain reflected right there on her face.

"You don't need me chiming in. You already know they're right."

"Fuck." In his head, the word came out loud and biting—a curse against himself, against the world, and most of all against Sofia. In reality, it was barely audible, and he sank back into one of the desk chairs, wondering when in the hell everything around him had begun to spin out of his control.

"I'm so sorry, Stark. I bollucksed that all up."

"What?" Damien turned to Quincy. "What are you talking about?"

"I gave Sofia the polygraph, but I only asked baseline questions and then questions about the kidnapping. I didn't ask about the vandalism at Nikki's office. Didn't even occur to me."

Damien reached around with one hand and massaged his aching neck. "It's not your fault. That wasn't even on the menu. We didn't have any reason to think the kidnapping was related to the vandalism. Still don't." He rolled his head, trying to release the tension. "It's fucked up, but it's not your fault."

Quincy studied him for a moment as if uncertain. Then he settled into the chair next to Damien and leaned forward on the desk, his chin propped on his hand. "Why would she do this?"

So many reasons, Damien thought. Every one of which he'd foolishly believed had been relegated to the past or dealt with in her treatments. "Jealousy, for one. I have my kids. My family. And she doesn't have me. Plus, she had a miscarriage recently. That was probably a trigger."

"She's in love with you," Evelyn said. "She always has been. I'm sure she knows what she did was wrong, but her feelings got the better of her."

"*Got the better of her?*" Jamie repeated. "I thought she was supposed to be all sane and stable now. Clean bill of mental health and all that."

"Maybe she is," Ollie said, returning from the kitchen with a basket of muffins. Behind him, Bree led Kari down the stairs.

"Um, hello? News flash. She totally tagged Nikki's office." Jamie looked to Ryan. "Right? I'm right, aren't I?"

"I don't know," Ryan said. "But I've been around long enough to know that she's smart. IQ off the charts, right?"

Damien nodded.

"So why didn't she pull the security feed from Nikki's building? She had to know it was there?"

"Maybe she knew she couldn't be identified," Ollie suggested. "The angle's wrong. That's why we couldn't get her face until we got the security vids from the alley."

Quincy nodded. "All true. But if the second lobby camera had been working, we would have been able to identify her on day one."

"That's true," Damien said. "She must not have known about the cameras."

"Maybe she's the one who tampered with the second camera," Jamie said. "Because that was the one that would show her face."

Ryan shook his head. "It was out for over a week before the vandalism."

Jamie shrugged. "So? Maybe she planned it. I mean, remember what happened after Germany? She befriended Nikki using a fake name so she could toy with her and make her cut."

"A fake name?" Quincy asked.

"It was freaky," Jamie told him. "She had this whole persona going. I mean, she practically became Monika Karts. An actress, I think. Someone working in Hollywood. And she hung out in this coffee shop that Nikki used to go to on Ventura Boulevard, just down the street from her first office. And they got to talking. Nikki genuinely liked her. And then one day she goes to Nikki's office, supposedly for some friendly get together, and instead she dumps out all these seriously disturbing photos of Sofia and Damien. Then she gives her this antique scalpel set and—"

"That's enough," Ryan said, his eyes on Damien.

"It's okay," Damien said, shaking off the memory of that horrible time when he came so close to losing Nikki.

"Sorry." Jamie winced. "It's only that—well, all I'm saying is that Sofia's a woman who can handle some long-term planning."

"She was messed up back then," Damien said. "Really sick. And that's not her anymore." He drew a breath, hoping that was true. He believed it. The doctors believed it. But was it right?

"Are you sure?" Jamie asked, voicing Damien's own doubts.

He shoved the doubt away. "I am," he said, with as much force as he could manage. "She's been under the care of the best doctors for years, and they all signed off on how well she's doing. She's gone through a twelve-step program. She's doing okay."

"Um, did you miss the part about the vandalism?"

"That doesn't mean she's unstable or crazy," Ollie put in. "Maybe that's who she is."

Damien shot him a hard glance. "What are you talking about?"

Ollie shrugged. "People do stupid shit. They throw things. They have screaming fights. They cheat on their girlfriends. Some of them probably get pissed off at people they love and then pull out a spray paint can. That doesn't mean they need to be institutionalized. Maybe it just means they need to talk it out with whoever they're pissed off at."

"He's right," Evelyn said. "I won't deny Sofia has problems—we both know the hell she survived. But she's worked hard to get her head on straight again. I think this is a blip. Not a relapse. At least," she added, "I want to believe it is."

"Believe me, so do I." Damien rubbed his temples, trying to grab on to the small threads of hope that Evelyn and Ollie had dangled.

"What are you going to do?" Quincy asked.

It was the right question, because the truth was, Damien needed action. He needed to move. To do. He needed to fix what could be fixed.

He needed to grab some semblance of control in a situation where there was no real control to be had.

What was that saying? Fake it until you make it?

Right now, that's exactly what he felt like he was doing.

"First, I'm going to call the UK and speak to her doctor, just to confirm what we've been saying. Then I'm going to go see Sofia. Talk to her. Tell her I know and get her to tell me what was in her head." He drew in a breath. "I'm going to arrange for her to pay reparations—and then I'm putting her on a plane back to London."

He looked at his friends, nodding to himself as he re-ran that list in his head. "But all that's for tomorrow. Right now, I'm going to go find Nikki. And this time," he added with a look to Jamie, "none of you are going to stop me."

"Wouldn't dream of it," she said. "And for the record, it sounds like you've got a good plan."

Damn right he did.

He left them to finish up and let themselves out, then headed back to his bedroom, expecting to find Nikki. But she wasn't there.

Frowning, he moved on to the girls' room, then stopped in the doorway when he saw her. She was sitting on the window seat, backlit by the moonlight so that she glowed with an ethereal beauty. Anne was asleep in her lap, and his heart swelled at the image of the two of them together, kissed by the light of the rising moon.

He started to step into the room, but then he heard it. A low, sad sob. *She was crying.* She was curled up in front of a window holding their baby and crying. Because of him. Because he'd fucked up.

How could he have been so ridiculously naïve to think that she just needed time? How could time heal the kind of pain he'd caused? He was supposed to protect her, to keep her safe.

She'd put her trust in him, and he'd failed completely.

And, dammit, he didn't know how he was supposed to live with that.

* * * *

For almost an hour, he'd been punching the bag, trying to pound out his frustration. His anger. His fear.

Frustration that he'd walked away from Nikki instead of talking to her. Holding her.

Anger at Sofia for tagging the office. Anger at himself for being so blind as to not even consider that she might have done the vandalism.

And fear. He was so afraid that she wasn't better. That this was the beginning of another long, slow spiral into the abyss.

Again and again, his taped hands beat against the bag, his arms burning, his feet moving. Always keep moving, right? A lesson that worked equally well in fighting and in business.

He thrust out again, a tight, pounding jab punctuated by an uppercut. Then another fast jab. Another, and another. And on and on, because how could he stop? He had a mission, after all. To get it all out. To leave himself an empty shell.

To start fresh.

Only then could he apologize to Nikki. And somehow, some way, make it up to her.

It wasn't working. The anger still swirled. Along with a wretched self-loathing that was driving him harder and faster and—

"Hey."

He froze. *Nikki.*

"Everyone's gone or asleep." Her gentle, soft voice touched him like a caress. "I was looking for you."

She was still behind him, talking to him from the doorway as he faced the bag.

He didn't turn around. "I would have thought that tonight you'd just as soon not find me."

He heard the soft pad of her feet on the mat, then saw her appear in the mirrors that lined the side walls. He watched, his already fast heartbeat picking up tempo as she approached, then pressed her hand lightly to his shoulder. "Is that how you feel about me?" she asked. "When I do something that pisses you off. You'd just as soon not find me?"

A smile tugged at the corner of his mouth. "Baby, how could you ever piss me off?"

Her sweet laughter was a gift he didn't deserve.

"Liar," she said. "And you don't have to answer because I already know the truth. You're always with me, Damien. Even when we irritate each other. Even when we think that we've destroyed everything."

He drew in a breath, amazed that she could find her way so easily through the noise and slide straight into his soul.

She moved around to stand beside the bag, facing him. "Here," she said, placing her hand over her heart. "That's where you are. In my heart and right beside me. Always, Damien. Even when it's dark and scary. Even when we fight, Damien. Even then, you're always beside me. Don't you dare believe it's different with me."

He looked at her. Just looked, taking in everything about this woman who was his. Who belonged to him so completely. A woman he didn't deserve, but knew he could never lose. The moment he lost Nikki was the moment he left this earth, because losing her would be to lose his heart.

She'd washed her face, and there wasn't a trace of makeup left. Her hair was pulled back into a ponytail. She wore one of his old Wimbledon T-shirts, the hem hitting her mid-thigh. She looked young and fresh and alive and earnest, and he wanted to pull her close and kiss her sweetly. He wanted, somehow, to make amends. But he didn't know how.

Despite her words, he didn't know how.

"I screwed up, Nikki." He pounded one more time on the bag. "I missed it. Ignored it. Was fucking blindsided by it. I wanted so desperately for things to be okay between you and Sofia that I didn't consider the possibility that even with the doctors giving her a gold star for mental health, that she was still a woman who would be jealous of my wife. Who might do something vindictive and stupid. I didn't see it, baby, because I didn't want to see it, and I'm so damn sorry."

"No." She shook her head as tears flooded her eyes. "No, Damien, I'm the one who's sorry. She's your friend, and you have a lifetime of history with her. You love her. Not the way you love me, but she's part of you, and I know how much having us at odds hurts you. And you thought she was better. Her doctors even told you she was better. Of course you trusted her."

She drew a breath and offered him a wobbly smile. "I'm sorry I said that you were wrong to trust her. That was wrong. Me lashing out in anger, and I'm sorry."

Her words, so sweet and heartfelt, moved him more he could ever express. But they were empty words, no matter how much she might believe them. The bitter truth was that her anger had been justified. He'd fucked up, and Sofia had hurt her.

And how the hell could they ever get past that?

She stepped closer, then wrapped her arms around him, her head to his chest. "Come to bed," she whispered.

He bent, then kissed the top of her head, breathing in the clean scent of her shampoo. "Soon," he murmured. "I just want to get in a few more punches."

She stepped back, and the moment she was no longer touching him, he felt cold. Lost. "Are you sure?"

"I'll be right behind you."

For a moment she only looked at him, and he knew she could see right through him.

But how the hell could he hold her close and take comfort in her body when he was the one who'd hurt her?

Chapter Twenty-one

The irony, of course, was that back when Sofia told him about her recovery and her twelve-step program, he'd given her access to one of the suites at the Stark Century Hotel that he kept open for personal and corporate guests.

Which meant that he was housing the woman who'd harassed his wife in one of the most luxurious hotels in the country.

She opened her door the instant he knocked, looking fresh and happy. She'd changed her hair again. Now it hung in midnight black curls around her fine-boned face, each ringlet tipped with blue.

"Damien!" She threw herself into his arms, silently demanding a hug. He gave her a gentle squeeze, then released her, gesturing for her to step back inside.

"I'm ready to go," she said, indicating the purse on her shoulder. "Is Alaine meeting us somewhere? Or is he cooking for us?"

"Come on, Sofia. Back inside. We need to talk."

Her brow furrowed, and he knew her mind was churning as she wondered what had happened and what he knew.

"What about brunch?"

"Canceled. I called Alaine on the drive over. Inside, Sofia. Now."

For a moment, he thought she would argue. Then she lifted a shoulder as if it didn't matter in the least. "Wanna order room service?"

"Later." He gestured for her to sit on the couch while he sat down on the chair opposite her. "Sofia, honey, why did you do it?"

"Do what?"

He just looked at her. And while he looked, her tears started to flow. "I don't know," she said, wringing her hands in her lap. "I really,

really don't know. I was lost, you know? I'd had the miscarriage, and even though I'm not ready to be a mom, it felt like everything was all wrong. Like I'd never have that. And I thought about you. And about her. And about how you have a family now and those little girls, and I was just sinking under, because I know that I'll never be to anyone what she is to you."

He remembered the violent anger sprayed across Nikki's office walls. He recalled the way she'd come to him later, asking if she could take over as the girls' nanny when Bree moved to New York.

A slow rise of anger pushed him to his feet and he paced, feeling the weight of her eyes on him. "Why did you show up at Nikki's office the other day?"

"I—I wanted to make sure it was all gone. And I wanted to apologize."

"I don't recall any apology."

"I couldn't. I'm sorry." She blinked, and more tears fell. "I'm a mess, Damien. The miscarriage—everything around it—I'm so sorry, but I'm a mess."

"And the father?"

She shuddered. "No."

"No?"

Her face went hard. "He's—just, no."

He stepped to the window, then looked out at the city spreading out below them. "I need you to go."

"Go?"

"Back to London." He turned to face her and saw panic in her eyes. "I'll arrange a flight and a flat," he added gently.

"That's it?" She licked her lips. "You're just sending me away? Like that'll make it all better?"

For a moment, he could only stand there, feeling so damned exhausted. Then he moved to the sofa and sat beside her, taking her hand.

"Come on, Sofia. Can you honestly tell me this isn't for the best? We'll always be friends, but it's not good for you and me to be this close together. You know that, right?"

She nodded.

"Do you really even want to stay?"

She shook her head, then wiped her eyes with her free hand. "No."

Her voice was low. Thin. "I want to get away so badly. But I didn't—I didn't know how."

"Just ask me. When have I not helped you? Even in the worst of it—"

"I know. You did." She wiped away a tear. "I love you, you know."

A fist tightened around his heart. "Sofia, please…"

"No, no, I don't mean—it's just that you're my best friend. I'm going to miss you."

"I'll miss you, too. And it's not goodbye. It's just distance."

She drew in a breath and gave him a shaky smile. "I know. Will you tell Nikki I'm really sorry? And I'll pay her back. Whatever it cost to clean up her office, plus some. I will."

"I know. You'll see your counselor when you're back in the UK? Promise?"

"Promise."

"Good." He kissed her forehead, then stood up. "Order room service. Whatever you want. Then pack your things. I'll arrange the jet and have Edward pick you up in a few hours. Okay?"

"Can I leave in the morning? I'd like—I'd like to walk on the beach. And maybe say a few goodbyes?"

He almost said no, but that was just because he wanted this chapter closed. Of course she should have the chance to say goodbye to the friends she'd made in the months she'd been in the States.

"Tomorrow, then," he said. "But I'm going to have Ryan assign one of his security team to say with you until you're on the plane. Fair enough?"

Her shoulders rose and fell. "You don't trust me."

"Should I?"

Her lips pressed together, and she studied her hands in her lap.

"Call me when you're settled."

"I will," she promised. And then, just as he reached the door, she said, "Thank you."

* * * *

Damien was relieved to have reached some sort of resolution with Sofia, but by the time he pulled up in front of the Malibu house, his friend was the last thing on his mind. Instead, his thoughts were on last night in the gym.

He'd been such an ass. Too lost in his own pain to realize that she'd thrown him a rescue line and was offering to pull him out of the mire. To hold him close and make it better.

All he'd done was push her away.

He needed to make it up to her, but other than finding and destroying Anne's kidnapper, he didn't know what would be enough.

So many fuck-ups on his shoulders, and he didn't know how to make it all right. He felt lost, and he never felt lost. Unsure, and he never felt unsure.

And he felt alone. Because even though he had the most incredible wife a man could hope for, he'd pushed her away. All because he was an arrogant fool.

He parked the car in the drive, then killed the engine. But instead of getting out, he clutched the steering wheel, bent his head, and let himself drift away on an ocean of self-recrimination.

He didn't know how long he stayed like that. All he knew was that he was jolted from his roiling thoughts by the familiar chime of his phone—a chime that signaled a text from Nikki.

The feathered edge of hope brushed lightly against him, and he checked his phone, smiling as he read the message.

Good morning, Mr. Stark. There's brunch waiting for you in the bungalow.

The words, so simple, were like sunshine to his heart. More, they were like a mirror reflecting back a truth that he didn't want to see—that as smart as he might be, sometimes he missed the mark by a mile.

Did he really think that he was the one taking care of her? That was bullshit. Nikki was taking care of him.

And how he'd ever survive a day without her, he really didn't know. Frankly, he didn't intend to find out.

He walked down the unpaved drive that ran from the front of the house down to the beach and the bungalow, passing the main door to go around to the deck on the back, expecting he'd find his wife there. Instead, he found a house that appeared to be completely closed up. The blinds were down, the windows shuttered. As far as he could tell, the bungalow was quiet and empty.

He checked the text again, but she'd definitely said the bungalow, and now he hurried to the door, not entirely sure if it was anticipation that was making him hurry or the fear that something was wrong.

He punched in the code, pushed open the door, and knew immediately that there was nothing at all to fear.

On the contrary, he'd just stepped into someplace magical.

As far as he could tell, every surface in the kitchen and living area was covered in white candles. Every surface, that is, except the kitchen island. The only thing on the island was his wife, stretched out like an offering, and completely naked.

"Nikki."

Her name was little more than a breath. A quiet prayer. A heartfelt thank you.

She was beautiful. Her hair gleaming. Her skin glowing golden in the flickering light. Shadows dancing over her in a way that his fingers envied.

"Baby, this is..."

He trailed off. Rarely was he at a loss for words, but right now, his vocabulary had abandoned him.

"I told you there was brunch," she said, and spread her legs just a little, making his body ache with a sensual craving.

He took a step toward her. "It looks absolutely delicious." He put his hands on her ankles, then gently stroked his palms up to her thighs, spreading her legs as he did. He tugged her gently closer, watching the way her body slid toward him on the polished countertop.

But then, as he started to bend, desperate to taste the feast between her thighs, she pulled her legs together, then propped herself up on her elbows, her expression managing to be both serious and teasing. "Don't get too excited, Mr. Stark. Not a single taste for you until you stop shutting me out. And don't even try to deny it."

"I wouldn't dream of it," he said, amused. He trailed a finger up her leg and side, grazing her breast as he circled the island, then went to sit on the couch on the far side of the living area. "Come here."

She turned her head to the side, looking at him, and said nothing.

"Nikki. Come here."

He saw the hint of a smile playing on her lips as she slowly sat up, then slid off the island. She'd tossed her white robe over the back of one of the kitchen chairs, and now she reached for it.

"Oh, no," he said. "If I'm going to spill my soul, we're doing this my way."

"Are we?" She tilted her head, studying him. "What's your way?"

"You straddling my lap so that I can see your face when we talk. And naked will work just fine."

"That's it?"

He matched her grin. "No, but it's a start."

"Hmm." She walked slowly toward him, then climbed onto his lap, her knees on the couch, tight against his hips, and her hands on his shoulders. "I think I've lost control of this intervention."

"Is that what this is?" he asked.

She brushed a kiss over his lips. "It is. I'm worried about you."

"You're worried about me," he repeated, then cupped her face. "Baby, don't you remember? You cut. For the first time since we've been together you took a blade to your skin."

"I did," she said. "And the circumstances were horrible. I was afraid and off-balance and the world was spinning out from under me. But you got me through it, Damien." She pressed her forehead against his. "And you can't use my cutting as your excuse."

He felt himself tense, her words hitting a little too close to the truth. "What are you talking about?"

"It's an intervention, remember? I'm talking about you. Tell me what's in your head, Damien. Because our daughter was kidnapped and it turns out her kidnapper wasn't acting alone."

He swallowed, but said nothing.

"The world's spinning away from us, and don't tell me you're handling it. Because I know you are. So am I. But it still hurts."

She kissed him lightly. "Add in that I cut and that the woman you suffered through your childhood with vandalized my office, and I'm going to go out on a limb and say that you're having a whole series of pretty crappy days."

He actually laughed. Even though it felt as if a fist was squeezing his chest, a strangled laugh bubbled out. "Yes," he said, because everything she said—every word, every syllable—was an echo of his thoughts.

She brushed his forehead with kisses. "Talk to me."

"Christ, baby, what do you want me to say?"

She shrugged. "The truth."

The truth. "Hell, where do I even start?"

"The beginning?"

He met her eyes, nodding. "That would be you."

"Me?"

"And Dallas. I saw you that night on stage. A beautiful woman in an elegant dress. And I wanted you so damn bad. And I got you. Because you're what I wanted, I made it happen. You're mine, Nikki, because I wanted you to be."

"I think I might have played a small role."

"Maybe." He allowed her a half-smile before continuing. "But this…" Christ, it was hard to even get the words out. "Baby, I don't know if we'll ever find this guy. Not ever. And the force of my will isn't worth shit. I can't just make it happen. I can't make it be over, the bad guy caught, our family safe, simply because that's the way I want it to be."

Her brow furrowed as she studied him. "You said this was about me," she whispered. "Damien, do you think I'm under some illusion here? You're a force of nature, sure, but I don't expect you to beat back the storm." She clutched his hand. "What I need to know is that you'll be there to help me weather it. You're my strength, Damien. But that doesn't mean you have to be strong all the time."

"You cut, baby," he said again. "The man we thought was behind Anne's kidnapping was shivved. And a woman I trusted—who I let back into our lives—trashed your office. Jesus, Nikki, why the hell would you ever trust me again?"

"Do you think my trust in you is that fragile? That it's illusory? Do you really believe that learning there's another kidnapper erases everything? It doesn't. Or that what Sofia did makes it all just go away? No way. Not even close. I trust you, Damien. I have from the moment I met you. You know that."

She pressed her palm over his heart. "You know it here, and don't tell me that's not true, because I'll know that you're lying. But if you want me to prove it, I will. Anything you want, any way you want it. Do you want to take me to Masque and strip me bare in the living room? Fuck me in front of all the other guests at the club? Do you want to take me to one of the clubs where Ryan takes Jamie? Whatever you want, Damien. Anything you want. I'll go as far as you want to take me, and I'll always trust you to bring me back again."

Dear God, she filled him up. He looked at her, feeling as if he would burst with love for her. Need for her. Gently, he cupped her face, then slowly moved his hands down, stroking her breasts, teasing her nipples, watching her face flush and her lips part.

Lower and lower until he cupped her sex, then stroked her gently as his fingers grew more and more slippery.

"Damien." Her voice was heavy with passion, so heated it made his cock ache.

"I thought about a portrait," he whispered.

Her eyes had fluttered shut, but now she looked at him, confusion on her face.

"That trust you said you'd prove to me. I thought I might want a portrait of you."

"I think you have one. You paid a pretty penny for it."

"Mmm, no. I mean a photograph. I thought Wyatt could take it. One of his erotic images. You, naked. Your legs spread wide, your fingers dancing over your clit. And your eyes looking straight into the camera, bold and sexy as hell."

"Oh." She licked her lips. "That's what you want?"

"For me," he said. "A portrait of my wife just for me."

"Okay." The word was soft, but the thrill of it spread through him.

"Okay?" he repeated.

She swallowed. "Call him now. He'll make the time for you. He'd come over in a heartbeat."

"He probably would. You'd agree to that?"

She nodded. "I told you. I trust you."

"And I love you," he said, then kissed her, slow and sensual, his fingers teasing her sex in time with the motion of his tongue. "So no."

"No?"

He shook his head. "It's a nice fantasy, but no. Wyatt's a friend. It would be too strange for you. I think that crosses a line."

He watched as relief washed over her. "And that, Mr. Stark, is why I trust you."

She started to unbutton his shirt as he let his hands roam free over her naked body. "Tell me, are there candles in the bedroom, too?"

"There are."

"In that case, I think it's time I made love to my wife."

"Yes," she said, her eyes looking deep into his. "I absolutely think it is."

Chapter Twenty-two

"This is excellent," Quincy was saying to Bree when Damien crossed the open area Monday morning, Lara clinging to his back like a monkey.

"What's excellent?" Nikki asked, putting a wriggling Anne down and aiming her toward the kitchen.

"Choca-pipcakes!" Lara squealed as Damien disentangled her, and Moira reached for her.

"Those are excellent," Damien agreed. "But I think Mommy was talking about something else."

"For bekfast, Daddy. Please? Choca-pipcakes!"

"Give Mommy and Daddy a minute with Miss Bree and Mr. Quincy, and we'll see."

"Come on, girls," Moira said. "We can get all the ingredients ready for your daddy."

"Pipcakes?" Quincy asked, once the chaos had settled and Damien and Nikki were able to cross to his workstation.

"A rare delicacy. Although not even close to bangers and mash or blood sausage."

"Insult my heritage and I won't share Bree's good news. Actually, I won't share it anyway. I'll let her do that. Bloody brilliant detective work, first time out of the gate, too."

Bree's cheeks bloomed pink from the praise, but she sat up straight, the picture of professionalism. "My parents always gave me grief for spending too much time on the phone in high school, but I developed some mad skills, and I've been living on the phone all weekend."

"I'm guessing it paid off?"

"Well, I think so. It's only—"

"A lead," Quincy said. "Our first, but not only," he added as Ollie walked up.

"One of Rory's coworkers told me about a girl he was fostered with for a while. I don't know her name, but I guess he really cared about her. Not romantically, I don't think. But like a sister. Again, I don't know exactly what was between them. But this coworker—Dan—said he was sure Rory sent her money a few times. And it may have been a regular thing. This is all gossip, right? But I figure if he's sending her money maybe there's a blackmail thing going on? Something that happened with him and her back when they were both fostered?"

"I'm going to see if I can get the record of his foster homes and foster siblings through channels," Ollie said. "And if not, I figure Ryan should be able to manage to get the records."

"It may not turn into anything," Bree said, her shoulders rising. "But—"

"It's excellent work," Damien said. "Exactly the kind of detail that lead to answers."

"Absolutely." Beside him, Nikki squeezed his hand. "Great work," she said, then stood to answer the house phone.

"It's Edward," she said a moment later, handing Damien the handset. "And Abby's here. She's heading in and wants to see both of us. Good work again, Bree," she said as she headed for the stairs. "I'll be right back."

"Did Sofia get away okay?" Damien asked his driver as he shot Nikki a thumbs-up.

"That's why I'm calling, Mr. Stark. I'm with Mr. Howser, the security that Mr. Hunter assigned, and it appears that she left the suite through the maintenance and housekeeping entrance off the kitchen while he was in the living area. We think she left right before I arrived, but we haven't been able to locate her."

Shit. "Thank you, Edward. I'll let Mr. Hunter know. Tell Howser to stay put."

"What's going on?" Ryan asked as Nikki and Abby approached.

"Sofia," Damien said. "She gave Howser the slip."

As Ryan cursed and stepped away, his phone in his hand, Damien pulled out his own phone. He dialed her number, not surprised when it went straight to voicemail. "Dammit, Sofia," he murmured as he opened the tracking app she'd agreed to months ago that would let him see the location of her phone. *Nothing.*

"She turned off her phone." Not that he was surprised. Sofia was far from stupid. If she wanted to run, she certainly wouldn't want to be tracked.

Quincy came over. "What happened? Is she okay?"

"Sofia?" Abby said. "The girl who visited you at the office?"

"The girl who tagged the office," Damien said gravely as Abby's mouth dropped open. He caught a glimpse of Quincy, whose expression was as dark as a building storm. "What?"

Quincy just shook his head. And before Damien could ask what the hell that was about, he turned and walked away.

Nikki slipped an arm around Damien's waist. "She probably just didn't want to be told what to do. Maybe she only wants to prove that you can't control her completely. She'll probably turn up tomorrow with an apology and tell you she got LA out of her system and is ready to go back to London."

"Maybe," he said. "But I intend to find her before then."

"Already on it," Ryan said as he returned. "I've got a team at the hotel looking at the security video in the elevators, stairwells, lobby, and garage. We'll figure out where she went and in what type of transportation."

"I know you will."

"Damien—" Ryan's voice was tight, and he ran a hand through his hair. "Howser's actions weren't up to standard, and that falls on me. It won't happen again."

Damien looked at his friend, a man whose skill and attention to detail had not only put him on Damien's radar all those years ago, but had formed the foundation of their friendship and Ryan's rise in the company.

He thought of all the mistakes he'd made himself since Anne's kidnapping. The wrong choices, bad judgment calls, and misplaced faith. He'd be one hell of a hypocrite to bring Ryan down a notch for not having complete and total control over his men.

"It's okay, Ryan," he said, intentionally using his friend's first name. "I've never doubted your ability or your follow-through. I know you'll handle it just fine." He shifted his attention to Abby, dismissing Ryan's apology as so much fluff, and saw the hint of a smile touch Ryan's mouth. "Should we head to the kitchen where we can talk easier?"

"Actually, I was hoping I could get everyone involved," Abby said, looking around the room. "Or at least as many of you as are willing to help."

"We got the prototypes in," Nikki explained, referring to the colorful, plastic encased GPS trackers that were the main feature of the upgrades rolling out soon as part of Fairchild & Partners' Mommy's Helper app.

"We've done some tweaks to the refresh rate—Travis is brilliant, I have to say—and we've also added the step counter. Next iteration will include a passive listen-in, but we're still working on the underlying tech."

"Listen in?" Bree said.

"Yeah, so, like, if your kid is being bullied at school, you can actually stream the sound around them."

"That's really cool."

Abby nodded, looking giddy. "I know, right?"

"This app is Abby's baby." Nikki flashed Abby a pride-filled smile. "And she's done an amazing job."

"I just want the roll-out to go smoothly, and I'm nervous. We have our beta testers lined up, but I want to use all of you as alpha testers for one particular issue we need to resolve. We're having some addressing problems—showing the tracker one house over on the app's map, for example, which would suck if you're trying to figure out where little Johnny is."

She grimaced. "I know it's a pain, but you just have to wear it on your waistband or bra for forty-eight hours. And keep your phone with you. The app won't actually be useable yet—so don't dump the kids at the Beverly Center and assume you can track them. You'll only be able to see the location of your own tracker in the analytics app, but right now, that's the only information I need."

She looked imploringly around the room. "Okay? Do you mind?"

Ryan grinned at her, then smiled up at Jamie, who was coming in from taking a phone call outside. "We're happy to, aren't we, babe? And so are these guys," he added, waving a hand at the tech team hunched over laptops as they crunched data.

"I have no idea what we're talking about, but sure."

"And you know Damien and I are in," Nikki said, and he nodded agreement, then added, "I'm sure Quincy will be, too."

"And me," said Bree. "And Moira and the kids. If you need more, I could ask Kari. The manager at Upper Crust. She's coming over tonight with more muffins."

"You two are going to spoil us," Nikki said. "Not that I'll turn down her chocolate chip muffins."

"Who would?" Abby asked. "And yeah, that would be great. I'll leave a few extras for her and anyone at the bakery who's up to helping." She glanced around the room, smiling. "Seriously, thanks. I'm just so nervous about this roll-out. Nikki can email everyone the link to download the analytics app and set up your account."

"It's going to be terrific," Nikki said, clipping the tracker to her waistband. "Eric's all over the ad campaign?"

Abby nodded. "We're good. The PR team is coming to the office on Tuesday."

Nikki glanced at Damien, and he nodded, then attached his tracker as well. They were looking for a needle in a haystack, and while he wasn't willing to scale back the hunt yet, there was no reason Nikki should miss her meetings. But until they found Sofia, he'd make sure that she went back and forth to work with two or three of Ryan's best men.

"I'll be there," she told Abby.

"Great. And tomorrow night, right?" This time the question was directed at both Nikki and Damien.

He shrugged, then glanced at Nikki, who looked equally clueless.

"Dammit, this is my fault," Abby said. "I meant to have Marge call you, but it must have slipped my mind."

"What's going on?" Nikki asked.

"Bijan is in town. He wants to meet for dinner."

"Oh." Nikki's eyes shot to Damien's. "We can do that, right?"

"Of course." Bijan Kamali was one of the principals of Greystone-Branch, Nikki's biggest client aside from Stark International. A client that had been hard won during the traumatic months surrounding her miscarriage. And Damien knew how much the continuing relationship with Greystone-Branch meant to Nikki. "When and where?" he asked Abby.

"Oh, good." The younger woman's shoulders sagged with relief. "I was afraid I'd have to handle it. I'll text you the time and place, okay? I'm guessing around seven."

"That'll be fine," Nikki assured her.

"Okay. Um, do you want me there, too?"

Damien bit back a smile as Nikki's eyes widened. "Of course. We're partners, right?"

Abby's face lit up. "I know. Sometimes it doesn't seem real."

"It's real," Nikki said as she slipped her hand into Damien's, "and I couldn't do it without you."

* * * *

"Not in the water, girls," Damien called as he walked along the beach with Nikki's hand in his, the girls running along in front of them.

They'd pigged out on chocolate chip pancakes, and now both little girls were bundles of sugared-up energy.

"This is nice," Nikki said, swinging their hands as they walked. "I want answers, don't get me wrong. But I miss having our house to ourselves."

"Do you want me to kick them out?" He could easily move the command center to Stark Tower, but he wanted to be involved. And if the team was in the Tower, he'd be living out of the apartment. And he wasn't willing to live without Nikki and the kids, so...

She started laughing.

"What?"

"You. You're completely transparent."

His brows rose. "On the contrary. I have a reputation for being a killer in negotiations precisely because I'm unreadable. And I'm one hell of a poker player, too."

She pulled him to a halt and hooked her arms around him. "Maybe to everyone else. But I see you clearly, Mr. Stark."

"And thank God for that."

She tilted her mouth up to meet his, and he kissed her gently, then slid his arm around her waist. She sighed as he held her and they both stood there, watching the girls run along the surf's edge, chasing waves and picking up shells.

"I want normal again, Damien. I want it all back the way it was."

"It will be."

She nodded. "I think it will. This is going to sound crazy, but I feel like we're making progress. Like the vandalism thing with Sofia."

He took a step back, studying her face. "You think Sofia had something to do with Anne?"

She shook her head, and he exhaled, realizing in that moment how much he'd feared that she believed exactly that—and afraid that deep down he was weighing that possibility as well.

"No, no. And I'm so angry at her for what she did to the office, and so sad for her as well—but it's an answer, you know? Not about the kidnapping, but an answer." She lifted a shoulder. "I figure that counts for something."

"Yeah," he said. "I guess it does."

"Mommy! Daddy! Look!"

He grinned at her and took her hand as they caught up to their daughters. And for the next hour, Damien was no one other than a husband and a father. It felt good. It felt freeing.

And when his phone chimed with a text message — *Come back to the house. We have a lead* — it felt like maybe, *maybe*, they were finally reaching the end.

Chapter Twenty-three

They were ridiculously overdressed for the jail, but the plan was to go straight from the Men's Central Jail near downtown LA to dinner at Cut 360, a five-star restaurant located just down the street from Stark Tower. After that, they'd either crash at the Tower Apartment or head back to Malibu.

Considering the girls would both be fast asleep by the end of the evening, Damien was thinking that a night alone with his wife in the apartment sounded like an exceptionally fine idea. One night away from the chaos. A morning with coffee and quiet. Just the two of them and a few exquisite minutes where they could forget the drama that was swirling around them.

"Damien?" He looked up, startled to find Nikki looking at him. "Where were you?"

He cupped her cheek. "With you, baby. Always."

Her eyes warmed, and he knew she understood when she responded with a small, almost secret smile.

"They're late," Charles said, glancing at his Rolex. "You'd think a prison would be more prompt. They operate on schedules, after all."

"Hot date?" Nikki teased.

"As a matter of fact … no."

Beside him, Nikki burst out laughing. Charles rarely joked. And Damien wasn't sure if his levity was a good sign, or an indication that they were so far through the looking glass that the normal rules didn't apply any more.

Damien had wanted to bring Ryan or Quincy, but the lead they were following was the statement of Rory's cellmate, who'd faked a hot appendix in order to get sent to the infirmary so that he could get a message to the prison investigators without any of the other inmates knowing. He'd insisted that he'd talk only to Damien, his wife, and his lawyer.

And that talk was supposed to have started fifteen minutes ago.

"You don't think..." Nikki trailed off. "I just mean, when we ended up waiting for Rory..."

"No," Charles said firmly, and Damien seconded the thought. The possibility that this informant had also been shivved before he could tell them anything was too horrible to entertain.

"He's probably just—"

The rattle of a heavy door being opened on the hall interrupted Damien. A moment later, they heard footsteps, then the key in the lock of the interview room door. A few seconds later, the familiar investigators stepped inside, a balding middle aged man with a pallid face stumbling between them, his hands cuffed together.

"You Stark?"

Damien nodded. "And you are?"

"Tim Blankenship. Used to own a garage. Now I'm working in the fucking laundry."

"I'm sorry if your skills aren't being well utilized," Damien said evenly. "But what does that have to do with me?"

"Not a goddamn thing," Tim said. He looked over his shoulder. "Just thought Heckle and Jeckle there could maybe find me a sweeter gig."

"Why don't you tell me what you know, and I'll think about putting in a good word."

"Sure, man. Sure. I can do that."

He fumbled to pull out a chair, then sat. Charles and Damien sat across from him, and though Damien indicated the seat next to him for Nikki, she shook her head and moved across the room, standing and watching Tim from a distance.

"Right. So I bunked with him. Not long. He wasn't here but, what? Just shy of a week? But he was a quiet guy. Leastways at first. After a couple of days he started talking more."

"What did he talk about?" Charles asked.

"Who the fuck are you?"

"Charles Maynard. I'm Mr. Stark's attorney."

"Right." Tim's head bobbed. "That's cool. And the piece?" He nodded toward Nikki.

"That's my wife, and I suggest you show a little respect."

"Hey, I'm the one's got the information."

"And I'm the one with the money and the power to make your life miserable if I don't like the tone you take with my wife. Are we clear?"

"Fuck you. Whatever."

"Tell me what you know and, as I said, I may be able to make your stay more hospitable. Turn into a pain in my ass, and I assure you that working in the laundry will be the least of your problems."

"Yeah, right. Whatever. Anyway, he started making noises about someone on the outside. Worried about them."

"Someone who meant him harm?" Damien asked.

"No, no, it wasn't like that. He wasn't making a lot of sense, honestly. Not even really talking to me. More like he was working something out in his own head, you know?"

"Did he say anything specific?" Charles asked. "Names, places? Anything at all?"

"Not so much. Said he had to keep his head down and his mouth closed to make sure she was okay. That she was taken care of and no one dropped the ball."

Damien caught Charles's eye. *That* was an interesting tidbit.

"She?" Damien repeated. "Did he tell you anything about this woman?"

"Not a thing. He just kept saying he had to keep his head down. He owed it to her. That she deserved better. Shit like that. Guy was quiet at first, but then honest to God, he was bugging in here. I mean, like the guy was not liking the bars for walls thing, you know? And I was seriously worried about his kidneys and his bowels, 'cause, man, that dude couldn't handle flashing his junk in public, you know what I mean?"

"I think I get the idea," Damien said dryly.

"He said that Stark would fix it."

"He said that?" Charles asked. "What were his exact words?"

"What? Like I'm a walking tape recorder? I just remember that he said that Stark would fix it. That's it. That's all she wrote."

"And you have no idea what that means."

"Not a fucking clue. You're Stark, right?" He aimed his bloodshot eyes at Damien. "What's it mean to you?"

"Unfortunately, nothing," Damien admitted.

"But that's not my problem, right?" Tim asked. "I mean, I'm relaying valuable information. Ain't my problem if you don't know how to dis-interpret it. Am I right?"

"You're as eloquent as you are smart," Damien said. "And I'll see if there's anything I can do to improve your situation. We really do appreciate the help, however cryptic it might be."

"Man, whatever."

The officers led him back to his cell while a prison liaison escorted Damien, Charles, and Nikki back to the main reception area.

"There's some woman he's been taking care of," Nikki said slowly. "And someone else was looking after her when Rory was in prison."

"Makes sense," Charles said. "Said he had to keep his head down. That he didn't want anyone dropping the ball."

Damien nodded thoughtfully. "But there's no reason I would care—no incentive for me to step in and fix it—unless this woman and her caretaker were somehow related to Anne's kidnapping."

"He took the fall in exchange for someone promising to watch after his wife?" Charles suggested. "Girlfriend? Then he changed his mind and decided to get help. From you."

"Not a wife. A foster sister," Damien said, remembering what Bree had told them over the weekend.

"We know he was giving money to a foster sister," Nikki explained to Charles. "We just don't know who or why."

"Well," Charles said pragmatically. "I think we need to find out."

* * * *

The waiter finished clearing the dessert dishes, then topped off Damien's coffee, his expert gaze surveying the other five people at the table. "Will there be anything else?"

"I think that will do it," Damien said as Bijan raised his hand, signaling for the waiter to bring him the check.

"Absolutely not," Nikki said. "Everyone knows the client doesn't pay. That's what billable hours are for," she added, with the perfect combination of humor and firmness.

Damien rested his hand on her thigh, his smile full of pride. She'd attended many business functions with him, but this was one of the few at which he was the extraneous party. And it had been absolutely delicious to sit back and watch his wife so competently handle the table. And so elegantly share the spotlight with Abby and Travis, making sure that Bijan and his husband, Laurence, knew that Abby was a partner in more than name only. And that Travis's tech skills brought significant value to their products.

"You're amazing," he whispered, sliding his fingertip along the hem of her skirt as he leaned over for the small pitcher of cream.

"I had a good teacher," she replied, making him grin.

"I'm so glad you were available this evening," Bijan said. "It was a whirlwind trip for Laurence and me, but I wanted to take the time to tell you how pleased everyone at Greystone-Branch is with your work."

"I'm always happy to make time for you. Especially when such lovely compliments are involved."

"We know we put you through the wringer a few times with last-minute software tweaks, and you never failed to step up to the plate."

"Travis took point for most of that," Abby said, and Damien noticed that she rested her hand lightly on his. "He's an incredible programmer."

"Abby's too kind," Travis said, pulling his hand free and reaching for his coffee.

Laurence cleared his throat, and for a moment, Damien wondered if he was going to comment on the tension between Abby and Travis. Damien had noticed it several times that night and in the office as well. Sooner or later, whatever was bubbling under the surface would explode, and that wasn't the kind of drama Nikki needed. Not on top of everything else.

As it turned out, though, that wasn't the drama that Laurence wanted to raise. Instead, he apologized for the timing of the dinner.

"I don't know how we missed the news," he said, his voice deep with compassion, "but we only recently learned what you went through with your little girl."

Beside him, Nikki stiffened, though this time, Damien was sure the tension was noticeable only to him. "Please don't worry," she said. "Anne is doing wonderfully. The house is a fortress, and she's home safe with her nanny and our best friends."

"We're both very glad to hear that," Bijan said as the waiter returned to hand Nikki the check.

"If you'll excuse me." Travis pushed back from the table, then started to thread his way to the men's room. Damien stood, excused himself, then followed. He waited outside the door, then pushed Travis back in as the younger man started to exit.

"I think we need to talk."

"Mr. Stark! What are you—"

"Are you fucking Abby?"

"Excuse me?"

"I think the question was clear, Travis. Are you fucking my wife's business partner? Because I'm a protective man, Travis, and the people who are important to my wife are important to me. That includes Abby. Frankly, that includes you, too. So I want to know what is going on between the two of you that might impact my wife's business."

"Nothing."

"I'm sorry, Travis. Have I not been making myself clear?"

"Nothing anymore," Travis amended, then sighed. "There's nothing. And there won't ever be."

Damien studied him. "Nothing or something, it's not my business unless it affects my wife's business. You two draw a line in the sand, you understand? And then you stay on one side or the other. Because if you don't, there's going to be trouble. And not just with me. You'll end up hurting her or she'll end up hurting you."

"I know. Christ, you don't think I know that?"

Damien backed off, some of the tension leaving his shoulders. "You want to talk about it?"

"No. Maybe. Not now." He scrubbed his palms over his face. "Did Bijan and Laurence notice? Did Nikki?"

"Nikki, probably." He grinned. "She doesn't miss much. But I don't think the Greystone guys did."

"Well," Travis said on a laugh as they headed back toward the table. "That's something."

What? Nikki mouthed.

"Later," he whispered as he pulled her chair out for her, then pressed a hand to her back as they headed toward the door.

Damien sent Edward a text, and as they waited for the limo, he and Nikki stood with the others at the valet stand. Travis left first, followed by Abby in an Uber. The valet was just pulling up with Bijan's rental car when a news van squealed to a halt and a cameraman and a reporter leapt out, the camera's light blinding.

"Mr. Stark! Mr. Stark! Is it true that you cancelled Rory Claymore's fellowship when he was in your program because of his relationship to Louisa Crenshaw?"

Damien hooked his arm protectively around Nikki, his first thought of *who the hell is Louisa Crenshaw* quickly replaced by the answer. *Rory's foster sister.*

"Damien? Nikki?" Bijan gestured toward his car, now ready to pull away from the curb. Damien shook his head. A nice gesture, but he wasn't going to bolt. Not like that.

"I suggest you check your facts," he said to the camera. "Mr. Claymore was a full fellowship recipient. He was never pulled from the program. Sadly, I don't count him among our successful alumni since he obviously considered kidnapping as a viable alternative to hard work."

"What do you say to the allegations that you're responsible for Rory's death in prison?"

"I'd say that as far as I know, you're the first one to make that allegation, presumably for ratings. But for the record, I'll add this—it's unfortunate that my daughter's confessed kidnapper was killed in custody. I would have liked the opportunity to better understand why he committed such a heinous crime. This, however, isn't the venue for speculation about his motives or his murder."

"Mr. Stark! Nikki!"

"We're done here," he said as Edward—timely as always—pulled to a stop in the middle of the street.

He got out, opened the door, then used an umbrella—on a decidedly clear night—to beat a path through the gathered crowd so that Nikki and Damien could slide inside, safe from the insanity.

"I'm so sorry, baby," he said.

"Don't be," she said, kicking her shoes off and putting her feet in his lap. "It wouldn't be a night out without cameras and obnoxious reporters. But if you want to make it better, Mr. Stark," she added, rubbing her bare foot over his crotch, "you just go right ahead."

Chapter Twenty-four

"Make it better," Damien repeated, cupping his hand over her bare foot, then sliding it up her calf, her thigh. "I might be able to manage that."

"Believe me, Mr. Stark," she said, "you already are." She leaned against the side of the limo, her arms above her head as she stretched, her lengthening body adding to the pressure against his cock.

"In light of Louisa Crenshaw, we need to get back home to the others." He reached the band of her panties, then traced his fingertip along it.

She made small circles with the ball of her foot, making his mouth go dry. "Not a problem. Malibu's a good forty-five minutes away. That sounds just about right."

"For what, Mrs. Stark?"

"For whatever you want. For however you're going to make the world outside this limo fall away." She met his eyes, hers so heavy with desire, he wanted to pull her into his lap and have her ride his cock all the way back. A hard, wild ride that left them both sweaty and sated.

Tempting...

But she presented so many temptations. And while forty-five minutes wasn't an eternity, it was time enough for more than a fast fuck. For that matter, it was time enough to play.

Gently, he slid her foot out of his lap. Then he lifted his hand up to the control panel and pushed the button to raise one of the jump seats, a set of recessed single seats that were available on demand for situations when the limo had more occupants than the bench seats along the sides and back could handle.

Not a feature he used often, but he had plans for it now, and as the chair rose mechanically from the floor, he slipped off the bench seat and moved to the single seat.

She frowned, then sat up. "Leaving me alone? Not exactly what I had in mind."

"No? You've been by yourself in a limo before. From what I understand, you enjoyed it very much."

He saw the spark light her eyes. "That was before I knew how much better it could be *not* being alone in the limo."

"Arguing?"

"Never. Sir."

He took off his suit jacket and tossed it onto the seat beside her. She glanced at it, then back at him in question.

"Fix me a drink, baby."

She took another quick, curious glance at his jacket, then moved the short distance to the wet bar, giving him a nice view of her ass as she bent to pour him a shot of Macallan, neat.

"Sir," she said, handing him the glass.

He downed the drink in one swallow, then put the glass down. "Make one for yourself if you want," he said. "Or sit back down."

She sat.

"Eager?"

She lifted a shoulder. "For what?"

He chuckled, letting his gaze roam over her, enjoying the view.

She'd worn a silk button-down blouse paired with a black pencil skirt and high-heeled pumps. She'd had a jacket at dinner, but she'd slipped it off the moment they'd entered the limo.

"Do you have any idea how perfect you were tonight? How much you impressed your clients?"

"Yeah?"

"Yes," he assured her. "You were amazing. And very, very sexy."

She laughed. "Not what I was going for." She met his eyes. "Except for you. Always for you."

"Prove it. Take off your shirt."

She held his gaze, then slowly unbuttoned her blouse. She wore a lace bra, and as she slipped off the shirt, he could see her nipples straining against the lace. His cock tightened, his blood pounding.

He breathed deep, feeling the buzz of the alcohol, and told himself to keep enjoying the show.

"Skirt next," he said, stroking his cock as she wriggled out of it, then sat primly back on the leather in only her bra and panties.

He let his gaze linger on her as he took in the gorgeous woman who was his wife. Who fired his senses. Who he still craved with as much heat as the first time he'd seen her, a heat that was supported by so much more. Love, respect, adoration.

That's what he wanted now. To adore her. To worship her.

"I can't," he said, watching with amusement as her brows rose.

"I don't think I've ever heard that before, Mr. Stark," she teased, making him laugh.

"No, that I can do just fine. I can't not touch you. I can't play like this. Not now. Not tonight." He held out his hand. "Come here, baby. I want to make love to you."

"Yes," she said. "Oh yes."

She knelt in front of him, helping as he tugged off his slacks and briefs. Then she straddled him as she worked the buttons on his shirt, not bothering to take it all the way off, but sliding her hands up his chest.

"Hi," she murmured, then kissed him. She was still in bra and panties. He was in a dress shirt. His mouth craved her, and his cock was aching with the need to fill her.

"I love you," she whispered, her fingers in his hair and her hips moving just enough to make him crazy. "And Damien?"

"Yes?"

"I want you inside me."

Hell, yes.

"Take off your panties," he ordered, but she just shook her head.

"Push them aside. Please. I just want you inside me now."

Her words burned through him, and he slid his fingers into her panties, pushing the soft damp silk aside, his fingers finding her core.

She rose up, her eyes locked with his as he entered her—as she lowered herself onto him, then rocked, the motion causing the edge of her panties to rub his cock in a way that was driving him mad.

He pulled her close, his mouth claiming hers, his tongue mimicking his cock as he fucked her mouth in slow, sensual movements, their bodies as one. Her hands stroked his chest, and he cupped her ass, guiding her movements as a slow, lazy fuck that built into something wild and frenzied. Something he hadn't intended but couldn't deny he wanted after all.

Because with Nikki there was always passion. Always heat.

Always something wild and wonderful and untamed.

And when she trembled in his arms—when he came completely apart and exploded inside her—he knew that even more than all of that, there was always the most important thing of all.

There was love.

* * * *

"Got anything for me?" Damien asked as they reached the third floor and found Ryan still at the computer with Jamie curled up asleep on the couch. "A quick report and then you should really take your wife home. Or at least crash in one of the guest bedrooms. Start back fresh in the morning."

"Jamie can sleep anywhere," Ryan said with a grin. "Or haven't you met my wife?"

Damien laughed, because Jamie pretty much *had* slept anywhere— and with anyone—until she settled down with Ryan. "Even so."

"We'll go…but I'll be back early. I'm expecting some video footage. Hopefully I'll have a link bright and early."

"You have found something. Tell me." He sat down, pulling Nikki into his lap.

"We found the girl. Rory's foster sister. Louisa Crenshaw. You can thank the asshole reporter for giving us a name. Saved tons of time. And yeah, she fostered with Rory for three years. She's an addict—currently in recovery—and she's got some pretty heavy duty medical issues, too. She's been living in a rehab facility and Rory's been sending her money weekly to cover the facility charges and her medical bills."

"Let me guess," Nikki said. "The money's kept coming even after he ended up in prison."

"You got it. Only now it's money orders. Totally anonymous."

"You mentioned video footage," Damien prompted.

"Right. From the rehab. Private facility, good security. They're sending us their video archives for the last six months. That's all they maintain."

"That's incredibly cooperative," Nikki said.

"So far, they've been great." He shot Damien a glance. "They also

She shook her head. "I'm prepared, just late. And Sofia's in Santa Barbara," she added, warding off any potential protests. "All is good, right? Well, as good as can be expected?"

He had to nod.

"So I'd rather be in Coop," she added, referring to her cherry red Mini Cooper he'd given her before their marriage. "I'll be back this afternoon," she promised, then started toward the stairs.

He tugged her back. "I think I need one more kiss."

She flashed a teasing smile. "Well, if you really need it, I guess—"

But he didn't let her finish. He was too busy quieting her with his kiss.

When he finally let her go, he went back in to check on Ryan and his team of techies who were just arriving.

"I talked with the girl this morning," Ryan said, glancing up as Damien approached. "And if you bring me coffee, I might be persuaded to share the details with you."

"I'll get it," Jamie said, padding through the open area in a tank top and pajama bottoms. She grinned at Damien. "Thanks for the offer to crash here," she said. "We took the suite by the pool. And we took a dip in the hot tub before crashing." She sighed. "It was very relaxing."

"I know," Damien said dryly. "I've done some dipping there myself."

Jamie burst out laughing. "I do love you, you know."

"Back at you, James," he said, using Nikki's nickname for her BFF.

Ryan leaned back in his chair, his arms crossed over his chest. "If you're done flirting with my wife…"

"Give it a rest, Hunter," Jamie said. "You know I don't go for the brilliant, wealthy, handsome type."

Damien bit back a laugh as Ryan tumbled her into his lap. "Oh, kitten, you are so going to pay later."

She bit her lower lip. "Promise?"

"Get me my coffee, minx."

"Yes, Sir. Damien? Coffee?"

"I'm good." He met Ryan's eyes, but his friend only shrugged. "She's well-trained."

"The hell she is. I've met your wife."

They both laughed, then quickly sobered as Quincy joined them, coming up from the first floor guest suite he'd claimed.

"So where are we?" Quincy asked.

"Unfortunately, Louisa Crenshaw says she knows nothing about who's paying her bills, and I believe her. Also unfortunately, we don't have their security archive. It's maintained offsite and is technically owned by the umbrella corporation that operates a number of rehabs across the country."

"Which means we're buried in red tape," Damien said.

"Which means we're officially going through channels," Ryan said.

"And unofficially?" Quincy asked, and Ryan nodded toward the two tech guys, who were already banging away at their laptops, heads bobbing to whatever music was pumping out of their headphones.

"My guys are on it. No guarantees, though. The facility uses actual video tape. Nothing digital. And it's shipped to the central retention system. I don't know if they archive it digitally. If not, we're out of luck unless they let us copy the tapes. Of course, we could break in, but that may be taking things a little too far." He met Damien's eyes. "At least until we're sure we're all out of options."

"You're saying we have another option."

"That's exactly what I'm saying," Ryan agreed, and Damien knew his friend well enough to know that Ryan was more than a little pleased with himself. "I figure the odds are good whoever is paying probably visited her at least once, right? So I got the visitor logs, which includes a designation of who they were seeing and a picture of the visitor's ID. Those, thankfully, are kept on site. And the facility was kind enough to give me the files for the last three months."

"Which means we look and see who was visiting Louisa Crenshaw," Jamie said. "But so what? How do we know if the person we see on the log is our bad guy?"

"We'll figure that out as we go along," Quincy said. "First, let's separate out her visitors and see what we're left with."

"Good," Damien said. "I've got a few calls I need to make about The Domino and some other business, but I'll be back up to see where you are in an hour or so."

"No worries," Ryan said. "Go run the universe."

An hour later, his universe was humming along nicely, and he was heading back up from his desk on the mezzanine to check in with Ryan. He'd just stepped off the elevator when his phone rang. He pulled it from his pocket, saw that it was from Nikki's office, and answered.

"Hey, baby. What's up?"

"Mr. Stark? It's Abby."

"Call me Damien, Abby. We've been over this before."

"Is Nikki still there?" Her voice held an edge of panic that shot through him like ice water.

"What are you talking about?"

"Oh, God."

"*Abby.*"

"She didn't make the meeting. I thought maybe she forgot. Or maybe you guys had a break in your investigation and she forgot to call."

"She left just after eight." He strode into the open area, snapping his fingers to get Ryan's attention. "She should have been there by now."

Ryan stood, his expression grim. Beside him, Jamie paled.

"She's not," Abby said. "Do you think something happened to her? Was she in an accident? Do you think—"

"I don't know," he snapped, then immediately regretted the outburst. "I'm sorry. Abby, thanks for calling. I'm going to see what I can find out. Call me if you hear anything."

"Yes. Of course. You do the same."

He promised he would, then ended the call, but continued tapping buttons on his phone.

"What's going on?" Quincy asked, climbing up the stairs, in sweats and a T-shirt, his body damp with the exertion of a workout.

Damien held up his hand. And then, when he saw the notification on his phone's screen, his blood ran cold.

"Her phone's off. I can't track her. *Fuck.*"

"What about Coop?" Jamie asked, and Damien almost kissed her.

"Brilliant. Yes. Of course." He'd had a tracker installed in Coop before he'd given it to her. He had one in all his cars as an anti-theft device, though for Nikki it was all about keeping her safe.

Now he pulled up the app, found the entry for Coop, and pressed the button to locate the car.

For a moment, he watched a wheel spinning on his phone screen then it stopped—exactly where it was supposed to be.

"Her office." He dragged his fingers through his hair, forcing himself not to panic. He never panicked. Panicking wasn't part of his nature.

But God help him, he was panicking now.

"On it," Ryan said, his voice sounding like it was in a tunnel. And then Ryan was there, standing in front of him, his hands on Damien's shoulders. "We have to assume this is tied to Anne's kidnapping. Probably the same perp."

"Oh, fuck," Quincy said, apparently catching up. "Bloody, buggered *fuck.*"

"I'll second that," Damien said grimly, pushing the panic down. Forcing himself to concentrate. Nikki needed him. *Him.* The man who'd been instrumental in getting their daughter back. The man who controlled billions and ran an empire. The man whose will was a goddamn force of nature.

She needed the man she married.

Damien Stark.

Someone thought they could take Nikki? Someone thought that they'd get away with it?

Someone was fucking wrong.

And, goddammit, he was finding his wife.

"We need to find out who's funding Louisa Crenshaw," he said to Ryan. "And we need to do it fast."

"I'm open to suggestions," Ryan said.

Jamie hurried over. "I think I have an idea. Someone who must know."

Damien turned to her. "Who?"

"Morey Dilliard."

"Who?" Damien asked again, only this time Ryan echoed the question.

"The reporter who blindsided you outside the restaurant," she explained. "Who else could have told him about Louisa? He won't want to reveal his sources, but..." She trailed off with a shrug.

"You can convince him?" Quincy asked.

"My wife can be very persuasive," Ryan said.

Jamie rolled her eyes. "No way will he tell me. But I think I know someone who can get him to share. Let me make some calls." She hurried off, her phone in her hand.

Damien met Ryan's eyes, but Ryan just shrugged.

"All right," Damien said. "What else have we got?"

"I think we're back to the clinic's visitor logs," Quincy said.

Ryan nodded. "Grunt work, but maybe it'll pay off."

"It has to," Damien said fiercely.

With the file split between the three of them, they started poring through the clinic's data, dumping all of Louisa's visitors into a designated subfolder that was rapidly filling up. The girl had a lot of visitors—doctors, friends, social workers.

"Mr. Stark," one of the techs—Jeff?—said right as Damien had finished a week's worth of visitor logs. "I've just finished reviewing the feed from Mrs. Stark's office parking garage. Her Mini-Cooper didn't enter the garage this morning."

"What?"

"I'm sorry, sir. I checked twice."

"But it's tracking to that vicinity."

"She must have parked on the street." Quincy said. "Or possibly in the lot behind her building."

"Christ." He ran his fingers through his hair. "I'm going to call Ollie. See if he can pull today's feed from their surveillance cam."

"Good idea," Ryan said as Damien stood to make the call, cursing when he got Ollie's voice mail. He left a message explaining what had happened and what he wanted, and hoped the other man would come through in time.

He returned to the workstation at the same time as Jamie, who held out her phone to Ryan. "Make it do the speaker thing," she said, waving vaguely toward the ceiling and the hidden sound system.

Ryan smirked, but hooked her phone into the equipment. A moment later, Damien heard Evelyn say, "Hello? Jamie, where the hell did you go?"

"She's here," Damien said. "We all are. You're on speaker."

"Apparently. Damien, I'm so sorry." There was no mistaking the grief and fear that colored her voice.

"I know," he said gently. "And I appreciate it. But right now—"

"Yes, yes. And I've got something for you. Not much, but maybe it'll help. Mr. Dilliard was reluctant, of course. But I convinced him to share a bit of info with us. Or rather, Matthew did."

"Matthew Holt?"

"The man has his finger in every entertainment pie in this city," Evelyn said. "And let's face it, that reporter isn't in the business of news. It's all about entertainment. So when Matthew assured him that if he didn't tell us what we needed, he might as well move back to Wisconsin and take up waiting tables, Mr. Dilliard believed him."

"Thank God. What do we know?"

"Still not much, I'm afraid. He didn't have a name. He only knows that the person who called to tip him off about Louisa and Rory was a woman. He checked out the facility that the woman told him about, found Louisa, and learned that she'd had past visits from Rory. That's all he knows. He swears."

"You believe him?"

"I do. Matthew does, too. I'm sorry it's not more helpful."

So was Damien. But all he said to Evelyn was, "It's something. Thank you."

"Anything you need, you let me know. You'll get her back, Damien. There's no other possible outcome."

He thanked her, then hung up and looked between Ryan and Quincy, his mind churning with Evelyn's words. *You'll get her back. You'll get her back.*

"Am I making a mistake not involving the police?" He asked the question bluntly. His mind said they were handling this exactly the way it needed to be handled. With experienced men and the best resources already in the thick of it and the ability to bring in more at a moment's notice. The police would only add red tape and slow things down.

That was what his gut told him, but he needed to be sure.

And so he looked between the two men he trusted and he asked again. "Is this team sufficient? Can we get her back? Or do I need to call in help?"

"We'll get her back," Ryan said with no hesitation. "At this point, law enforcement would only jam up the works."

The relief that swept over him was palpable. "Right. So Dilliard's tipster was a woman. Odds are she visited Louisa as well. Let's pull out all the men. That should narrow the field some."

"On it," Quincy said, and he started to flash the ID images of the various women on the projection screen as Damien rubbed his temples, his heart aching and his mind churning.

He couldn't lose her. Whatever happened, he couldn't lose her.

Conversation swam around him. Ryan talking with Jeff about possibly tapping into traffic cam footage. Quincy wondering aloud if a second call to Ollie would be a good idea. Behind him, he heard Bree offer the girls a muffin, and then the pounding of little feet as Lara and Anne raced into the open area squealing that they were getting muffins for snacks.

He bent down, scooping them into his arms, his gut twisting as he realized that he hadn't told Bree that Nikki was missing. She'd been down in the playroom with the girls when Abby's call had come, and it hadn't even occurred to him.

"Daddy? Whatsa matter, Daddy?" Lara asked, and since he couldn't answer, he just held her tighter.

When he could speak, he called Bree over, and she came with Kari, presumably thinking he wanted a muffin.

"Bree," he began, then noticed the way Kari was staring at the screen.

"Wait, go back," she said when the image changed.

Damien glanced back only for a second at the returning image, barely even registering the photo ID of a woman in glasses behind which she had eyes rimmed in thick lines of kohl. A mass of wild, curly blond hair covered most of her forehead, and her lips were painted in black lipstick.

Instead, Damien's attention was on Kari's face.

"You know her?"

"It's the same girl," Kari said. "I thought so when I was here the other day. On the video, I mean, but I wasn't sure. But that's her. That's definitely her."

Damien frowned, confused. He glanced at Ryan and Quincy, but neither of them seemed to understand either.

"The video?" he asked.

"She was in a parking lot. It was on the projection screen the other day when I was here. It took me a while to place her, but then I realized why she was so familiar. She's the girl who introduced me to Rory." She pointed at the screen. "Different hair and way different makeup, but that's her."

Damien turned, and this time he paid attention to the image on the screen. He ignored the heavily penciled eyes. The glasses. The unfamiliar hair and strange lipstick.

Kari was right. The woman in the visitor ID photo and the woman in the parking lot were the same.

And both women were Sofia.

A flood of nausea crested over him, and he rose to his feet, trying to battle it down.

"Mr. Stark?" Bree took a step forward as if to steady him, but he held a hand up, warding her off as he turned his attention to Kari again.

"You're sure? Absolutely positive?"

She licked her lips, looking more than a little intimidated. "Um, yeah. I'm sure. I even remember that one time she told Darla—you know, she works the register in the mornings—that she thought Rory and Bree would be a cute couple. I don't know. Maybe that stuck in my head and that was why I introduced them." She turned to Bree with a shrug.

"I don't get it," Bree said, tilting her head toward the video. "Who is she?"

"Sofia," he said. "And it doesn't make a damn bit of sense."

It would though. He pulled out his phone and dialed her number, but it went straight to voicemail. "Sofia. It's me. Call me back."

He hung up, then tracked her phone. Once again, the map showed that she was in Santa Barbara. Fine. If she was ignoring his cell calls, he'd get through to her on the house line.

He dialed again, this time ringing the hotel's front desk. "This is Damien Stark. Put me through to Richard Layton," he demanded, referring to the manager of the Pearl, who Damien had personally hired several years ago.

"Mr. Stark." Richard was on the line within seconds. "Is there a problem?"

"I need you to check a room. Sofia Richter."

"Oh. Of course. Are you calling about Ms. Richter's phone?"

A chill ran up the back of Damien's spine. "Her phone?"

"Housekeeping found it after she checked out. I was going to have it sent by messenger to your office. That seemed the most expedient way to return it."

"No. No, just keep it there. I'll have someone pick it up. Soon." He ended the call, his body numb. She'd left.

More than that, she'd obviously left the phone behind so that he would believe she was still there and couldn't track her.

So where the fuck was she?

And was she the one who'd taken Nikki? Or was he now thinking the worst of her, just like he'd earlier been thinking the best?

"Damien?" Ryan stood by his side. "I only heard one side of that, but she left her phone?"

"Send someone," Damien said. "Get them there fast, get the phone. Before this is over, we'll probably need to see what's in her contacts and emails."

"On it," Ryan said, signaling to Jeff. "Get Grayson here with a chopper. Five minutes ago."

"Done."

"This doesn't make sense," Ryan said. "You really think Sofia is behind the kidnapping?"

"I don't know." He paced the length of the open area, back and forth, his hands at the back of his neck. Bree and Kari, he noticed, had retreated back to the kitchen. "God knows she's got the intellect to pull something like this together, but I just don't see her doing it. And besides, she passed the polygraph."

"I'm not so sure she did." The words, low and edgy, came from Quincy, who was leaning against the workstation. His hair stood on end, as if he'd been running his fingers through it, and his expression was dark as thunder.

"What are you talking about?" Ryan asked. "You administered the test when she showed up after Anne's kidnapping."

"I did," he said. "But I didn't know about Monika Karts. I didn't know she adopted personalities. I didn't know about that aspect of her mental health."

"What the fuck does that have to do with anything?" Damien snapped.

"Polygraphs aren't an exact science," Quincy said. "But the bottom line is that they rely heavily on the physiological changes that occurs when someone lies. But someone with Sofia's history—"

"She becomes the person," Ryan said flatly. "She believes the lie."

"I've seen this before. Paris. Ten years ago." A flash of rage contorted Quincy's face before disappearing as quickly as it came. "Just like Sofia, and the bitch burned me to ashes."

"God*dammit*," Damien said, lashing out and kicking over the nearest table, sending a laptop and a computer tumbling to the ground. "This is all on me. I didn't give you the information so you could do your job. And I didn't look closely enough because she's like my family. My goddamn fucked-up family."

He collapsed into a chair, closing his eyes and forcing himself to breathe. To just breathe. "I can't lose her. Christ, Ryan, if I lose Nikki..."

"You won't." Ryan's voice was calm. Strong.

"The girls." Damien shot to his feet. "I don't want them to see me like this—"

"Jamie went to check on them and tell Bree the situation. She's taking them to the bungalow."

"Situation," Damien repeated. "What a fucking horrible word."

"We've got this," Ryan said firmly. "We just need to focus. We'll get her back."

"We will." He swallowed, once again pushing the fear away along with the self-recrimination. None of it would do her any good. He had to think. He had to act.

He had to find her.

"If Sofia is behind this, then she must have Nikki somewhere. We need to keep looking for surveillance footage. Find video of the grab, and who knows what else we'll learn."

"On it," Quincy said. "And I'll hook in Ollie."

"If she was planning this, there might be info in her phone. Get Jeff whatever support he needs to hack into it as soon as he gets to the hotel. Tell him to stay there so he's got access to a decent internet connection. We may need him to pull information for us. Let Richard know and get him set up with a space to work and whatever tech he needs."

"Done," Ryan said, pointing at the other tech guru, who nodded and hurried off to make the calls. "I have to say, though, I don't think she's behind this. Involved, maybe. But behind the kidnapping? I don't buy it."

Damien looked hard at his friend. "I don't either," he admitted. "But I want you to tell me why."

"Anne," Ryan said. "Nikki's a question mark. She'd certainly have hurt her in the past, and I'm not sure about now. But I don't see her hurting Anne."

"Anne wasn't hurt," Damien pointed out. "But Sofia was hurting. She'd had the miscarriage."

"Even so."

Damien nodded. "Honestly, I agree with you. But we both could be wrong. God knows I seem to be that a lot lately. Can't say I like the feel of it. And if we're right and she's not the one pulling the strings, then we're right back where we started."

"Except maybe there will be something in her cell phone. A contact. A call history."

"Maybe." The idea of waiting for Jeff made Damien's stomach twist, and he crossed the room again. Like a shark, he had to keep moving or else he'd die. Had to keep his thoughts churning. Had to keep chasing after whatever it was that he was missing, because there was something there. Something important. Something—

No.

Oh, holy fuck, no.

"Damien?"

Ryan's voice sounded a million miles away. He felt the blood drain from his body. And he heard the echo of his father's words—*And God, even Sofia. I actually went and added that poor girl to the mix. That's how low I sunk.*

He looked at Ryan. "What did he mean by that?"

Ryan's brow furrowed. "What did who mean?"

But Damien wasn't listening any longer. He had his phone out. He was dialing his father. And when Jeremiah answered, Damien wanted to reach through the phone and grab the bastard by the scruff of his neck. "What did you do?" he demanded, his words pouring out. "What did you get Sofia involved in? You weren't talking about the tennis circuit. That was all on Richter. You did something now, you fucking bastard. What did you do, old man? You tell me what the fuck you did."

"Breckenridge." Jeremiah's voice sounded lost. "She was alone. Broke. She was looking for help. And he said he'd let the money I owed him slide until after The Domino investment paid off. All I had to do was introduce them. That was all. She could have walked away any time. I just introduced them."

Damien's head throbbed. He tried to make sense of the words. "Sofia's been dating Richard Breckenridge?"

"I just introduced them," Jeremiah said again.

Suddenly, Damien understood. "The miscarriage. Breckenridge was the father."

"It's not my fault," Jeremiah said, but Damien barely heard him.

He ended the call and looked at Ryan. "He hooked her up with Breckenridge. All my life I've tried to protect Sofia, and my father introduced her to that perverted, abusive, misogynistic pig. He got her pregnant. He's probably hit her. God knows he's using her."

"And isn't fucking Sofia a stellar way to get back at you?" Ryan said, his voice harsh. "Almost as good as kidnapping your daughter."

"Or hurting my wife." He shivered, his body suddenly as cold as ice. "I have to go. I have to find him."

He started for the stairs.

"Go where?" Ryan called, but Damien didn't answer. Hell, he didn't know. He'd call Ryan from the car, get the team searching property records for Breckenridge's address. Right then, he simply had to move.

He got as far as the guard station and saw another car in the drive. A plain white Toyota. A rental. And there, in the driver's seat, was Sofia.

She looked up, her eyes meeting his through the windshield. Then she slammed open her door and raced toward him, collapsing at his feet as he bolted from his car.

"Damien," she cried. "I did a bad thing. I think I did a really, really bad thing."

Chapter Twenty-six

"What did you do?" Damien demanded, pacing in front of the chair where he'd parked her. "Sofia, tell me where my wife is."

He'd managed to hold his fury in check until he got her into the house. He'd been silent. Completely silent in the face of her sobs. He knew that if he said even one word—if he opened that gate at all—it would all spill out. And he couldn't let it. Not until they were inside. Not until he had help.

Not until he was sure he wouldn't fucking explode.

"I don't know," she said. "I swear, Damien, I don't know."

He clenched his fists at his sides. He'd never wanted to hit a woman, but dammit he wanted to hit Sofia now. And that reality made him both profoundly angry and desperately sad.

Ryan laid a hand on his shoulder. "Pull it back, Stark. We'll get there. But we need to give her space."

"Fuck space," Damien snapped, but he turned away, his hands clenched behind his neck as if that pressure could vanquish the urge to lash out.

Ryan crouched down until he was eye level with Sofia. "Did Richard Breckenridge organize Anne's kidnapping?"

Sofia nodded, her nose running and tears leaking down her face. She wiped a hand under her nose and sniffled. "I told him not to. I told him. But he said I should be glad. Because you didn't deserve what you had. And he said he wasn't going to hurt her. He was just going to scare you."

"Did you help?"

"No. Yes. I don't know." She licked her lips. "I didn't tell. I should have told. But then I did, but Damien didn't figure it out."

Ryan shot a glance toward Damien as he stood up, then looked back at Sofia. "You mean you did tell? I'm not following you. Can you explain?"

She shook her head. "I don't know. I don't know how to explain."

Quincy stepped forward. "We talked. Do you remember? I gave you the test? Hooked you up to wires. You told me you had nothing to do with the kidnapping."

"I didn't. Cross my heart." She drew an X over her chest with her fingertip as she talked. "That was Rory. That was all Rory."

"How did you meet Rory?" Ryan asked as Damien, finally calming, sat in a chair and watched the woman who was once his closest friend. Who'd been his responsibility for decades.

"I knew Louisa. We met at meetings. When I was in recovery and she was, too. And there was a boy who helped her. And when Richard needed someone to help him—someone who needed money…"

"You suggested Rory?"

"He needed money for Louisa. I didn't know. I swear. About Anne. About him wanting to hurt you. I didn't know. I just did what he told me. Because he was taking care of me."

The words shot straight to Damien's heart. *Breckenridge was taking care of her.*

Which meant that Damien hadn't been.

"He told you to spray paint her office?" Damien asked, his voice low as he worked to stay calm.

She shook her head. "I did that. I was angry about losing the baby. And because Nikki hadn't. But mostly because I wanted you to figure it out. I wanted you to catch me, because then I could tell you. Don't you see?"

Her eyes flashed with desperation. "Don't you get it? If you caught me, I could tell you everything. And then you would protect me. That's why I looked at the camera. The security one in Nikki's lobby. But you didn't find me, and then he took her and then it was too late."

"That camera was broken," he told her. "It took a long time to find out it was you."

"But that's not my fault." She looked at the three of them, almost vibrating with desperation. "That wasn't my fault."

"And you ran."

"He did bad things. I didn't think you'd believe me."

"So why did you come now?" Quincy asked.

She bit her lower lip, and heavy tears dripped from her lashes. "Because he made me help take her, and I didn't want to. And you love her." Her eyes when she looked at him were accusing. "Don't you?"

"More than anything."

A sob broke from her throat. "And I love you. So I can't do that to you. I can't. So I came here instead of leaving. I was supposed to go away. To hide until it was over. But I came here because I had to tell you."

He felt the weight fall from him, like water draining from a tub. "Thank you," he said. "You'll help me find her?"

She nodded. "Except I don't know where he took her."

"Maybe we can track him," Ryan said. "How did he get her?"

"I rear-ended her at a stoplight. He made me. And then when she pulled over, he took her."

"And then you drove her car to her office?"

Sofia nodded.

"What intersection?" Damien asked, and when she told him, he pointed to Quincy. "Traffic cameras," he said. "Maybe we can figure out his route."

"Working on it."

"Sofia, I'm not mad at you," Damien said. "Not anymore." He knelt in front of her, his hands on her knees. "I need you to think. Do you know where he'd take her?"

Her lips pressed together as she thought. After a moment, she nodded. "He has a house in the canyons. I don't think it's really his. I think it belongs to a friend. Someone rich who's never around."

"So no property records," Ryan said.

"And you don't know where it is?"

"Just that it's off Franklin Canyon. I've been with him, but he drove. I didn't pay attention. It's confusing in the hills. But I know the codes. For the security gate and the front door, I mean. I can get inside." She smiled, as if she'd just solved the problem, then her face crumpled. "Except I don't know where."

"Fuck." Damien paced, pounding his fist into his palm as he tried to think. He'd already tried tracking Nikki's phone, but he tried again, even knowing it would be futile. It was, of course. And tracking her car didn't help. If only he'd—

He turned to Ryan. "*Abby*," he said. And as Ryan stared in confusion, Damien called Nikki's partner, kicking himself for not remembering sooner.

"I need Nikki's log in for the Mommy's Helper analytics app," he said. "I need to locate her tracker, right now."

"Damien? What's going on?"

"Abby, just do it."

"Right. Sure. I have to get in through the back end. I'll text it to you."

He had the information in under a minute. He signed out of his own account then signed into hers. He held his breath, praying she hadn't left the damn tracker on their bedside table.

For a second, there was nothing. Then he saw the little red dot representing Nikki—and it was right there in Franklin Canyon.

"Come on," he said to Sofia. "You're going with me."

Chapter Twenty-seven

"Bloody fucking hell." Quincy sat behind the wheel of the black Range Rover, then glanced at Damien in the passenger seat. "This can't be right."

"No," Damien said grimly as he stared at the empty lot with the *For Sale By Owner* sign. "No, it can't be." He opened the passenger door and got out, Quincy and Ryan stepping out, too, along with Sofia.

The rest of the team—essentially a private SWAT team that Quincy and Ryan had pulled together—stayed in the Range Rover, with a second unit following behind. Only ninety minutes had passed since they'd tracked Nikki's signal, and that included travel time from Malibu. Damien knew they'd moved fast—knew that pulling this team together that quickly was a minor miracle, even though Ryan assured him that they'd been at the ready since Anne was taken. A new sub-group of the security division that he'd assembled.

All well and good, but ninety minutes was ninety minutes too long. And now they'd hit another goddamn snag.

"Is it here? In this lot?" Ryan looked around at the lot that sloped downward at such a steep angle it would take an engineering feat and a lot of money to build on it. "Did he find it and toss it?"

"No," Damien said, because even though Ryan could be right, that wasn't a possibility he was willing to consider. Because that possibility meant that they'd hit a wall. "No," he repeated, remembering Abby's words. "She said the trackers were having addressing problems, remember? Nikki's nearby. We just haven't pinpointed it."

"So we draw a circumference and go door to door," Ryan suggested. "Do that, though, and we tip him off."

"And that's still a lot of properties," Quincy said. "Everything adjacent to this lot. And then at least one more layer out beyond that. Even if we send the team out, it'll take time. And it's not as if we can storm every house. We'll have to assess, narrow the possibilities, and then hope to hell that when we do go in, we're right."

Damien turned to Sofia, who had crouched down to urge a caterpillar onto her finger. Now she stood, watching it inch along the back of her hand. "Would you recognize it if you saw it. The drive? The gate?"

"Maybe. I don't know. The gate was black, and there was a box for the code. But I couldn't see the house, and most gates look the same."

Damien bit back a curse. They were running out of time and ideas. If only her cell sent a GPS signal even if it wasn't turned on, then—

Not her phone. Sofia's.

"Call Jeff," he ordered Ryan. "Get him on the phone now."

"Damien?" Sofia came up behind him. "Did you find her?"

"No," he said. "You did."

She frowned, her gaze shifting to Ryan, whose face had just cleared. He obviously understood now, too.

"You've been there," Quincy said to her. "To the house?"

Sofia nodded.

"In that case, the location is probably—not definitely," he added with a warning look toward Damien, "—stored in the phone."

"It will be there," Damien said. "She hardly ever turns off her phone."

"Jeff's on the line," Ryan said. "He's in the phone and—yeah, that's right. Franklin Canyon." A pause, then Ryan looked at Sofia. "You visited a location near here about a week ago. Is that it?"

Sofia nodded, her eyes wide. "I had no idea you could do that."

"Most people don't," Damien said, as Ryan studied the map link that Jeff texted.

"There," he said, pointing to a property that was two lots over with no visible structure. Presumably, the house was set far back, behind the gate.

"I'm going in alone with Sofia."

"The hell you are."

Damien stood his ground. "Don't push me, Ryan. I have Sofia with me. She knows the house. Knows where he probably has Nikki. I get in, get Nikki out, then your team busts in and does your thing. Try to capture Breckenridge, but if you have to kill the fucker, then you do that."

"And if you're caught? Jesus, Damien…"

"Then I make him a deal. Release Nikki, and he can have me."

"No."

"This is the plan, like it or not. I'm doing what it takes to get her free. And you know damn well that you'd do the same."

Ryan ran his fingers through his hair, but didn't argue. Beside him, Quincy focused on Damien. "Take us through it."

"I go in with Sofia. Once we've confirmed the gate code, we relay it to the team, and you follow. You hold your position until I get Nikki clear. Other than that, use your judgment."

Quincy and Ryan exchanged glances.

"It's not up for negotiation," Damien said, then turned to Sofia. "Let's go."

"Wait," Quincy said. "You know how to handle a gun?"

Damien nodded, then took the Glock that Quincy handed him. "Don't hesitate," Quincy said. "If you need to, you fire."

"Trust me," Damien said, thinking of the bastard who had his wife. "I won't."

As she'd said, Sofia remembered the code, and as she punched it in, Damien texted it to Ryan. They were on foot, hoping that the lack of a car would better conceal their entry. Unfortunately, there was no way to get in other than the gate, as the fence surrounding the property was electrified, and Sofia knew that cutting the power would trigger an alarm.

"But I don't think he monitors the gate camera," she'd said. "I'm pretty sure the security monitors are in an owner's closet. And I'm pretty sure it's not his place. Some guy he knows who's mostly in Europe. Unless they own it together."

"Are you certain?" Ryan had asked, and she'd shaken her head.

Still, it was the only intel they had, so they were acting on it. Now, the two of them stayed off the driveway, walking across the landscaped yard to the house in the distance, barely visible because of the way the lot sloped downward, so that the house was essentially built on the side of the canyon and they were approaching the small part of the roof that was visible.

"There are stairs down to the front door," Sofia explained. "And then the house takes up five floors. Nikki's probably on the second floor. That's the media center, so there aren't windows."

"Let's go."

They moved slowly. Quietly. The weight of the gun in his hand providing some comfort. There'd been no ransom demand yet. And it occurred to Damien that Breckenridge probably believed that Damien didn't yet know that Nikki was missing. After all, if Abby hadn't called, Damien wouldn't become concerned until the evening.

The thought gave him hope. And he held onto that hope until they reached the media room. That's when he pushed open the door and walked in to face Richard Breckenridge, a gun aimed right at Nikki's face.

"Do it, and I'll blow your wife away," Breckenridge said, nodding to the gun in Damien's hand. A gun that was aimed at Breckenridge.

"I mean it," Breckenridge said. "You fire, and so do I."

Damien cursed himself for walking into a goddamn trap.

"Now put your hands in the air," Breckenridge ordered.

Damien did, his eyes fixed on Nikki—bound and gagged to a chair.

"Take that weapon from him, my dear," Breckenridge ordered Sofia, who took it from Damien, then scurried away.

"Did you really think she'd help you?" Breckenridge asked. "Did you really think it would be easy? Did you honestly believe when we had our little *chat* in your office that you were better than me? You? Because you're nothing, Stark. Nothing. Sofia knows it. That's why she's helping me. Because I want to hurt you, Stark. I want to hurt you where it counts. And that works out well, don't you think? Because the same thing that you love is something Sofia hates. Something she wants gone. Something—someone—who's been a thorn in her side for years and years. I know. She told me."

Rage boiled inside Damien. "You hurt my wife, and you are a dead man."

"Not really radiating the power today, Mr. Stark."

"Do you think I came alone?"

"Oh, your team. About that, I changed the gate code. Right after Sofia punched in the old one. And the fence really is electrified. They may get on the property, but it will be too late. Did you notice the helipad on the roof? Sofia and I will be leaving soon. But not until I kill your wife."

"I will hunt you down, you deranged fuck."

"I believe you. But your wife will already be dead no matter what you do to me. And besides, you won't find me. And if you try—if I get even the slightest wind that you're chasing me, have hired an assassin to come after me, anything clever like that—then I will make sure that your children die. Painfully. Might be an assassin's bullet. Might be poisoned food at school. But I'll get to them." He smiled. "Like I said. Not so powerful now, are you?"

"Kill me instead," Damien said. "I'm the one you want to get rid of. I'm the one standing in your way, who insulted you. Who hurt Sofia. Kill me. But please," he added, looking at Nikki who was shaking her head violently, her eyes pleading. "Please don't hurt my wife."

"Because you love her. Isn't that sweet? You love her, and you don't love Sofia. Sofia, darling, do you hear this?"

"I do love you," he told Sofia. "I always will. But not like that. You're the sister I never had. That's why I've always tried to take care of you, and I'm sorry if I failed. But, Sofia, you have to know. You have to see how it is between us." He swallowed, desperate to find some magic words that would save them. Save Nikki. But barring that, he had to at least speak the truth. Had to make sure that Sofia knew what she was destroying.

"She's my heart," he said aloud, his eyes on the woman who'd made his life complete. "She's always been in my heart, even before I met her. She's a part of me, Sofia. Nikki dies, and I die, too. Maybe that doesn't matter to you anymore. But it's the truth. Kill Nikki, and you've killed me as well."

"Romantic bullshit," Breckenridge said. "And I think we've had enough of it. Because as much as I'd love to stay and chat, your diligent team is working their little asses off to figure out a way in. And since they just might manage that, I think it's time for my exit. Sorry, Damien, but it's time to say goodbye to your wife."

"*No!*" Damien sprinted forward, aiming for Breckenridge, who had once again lifted his gun toward Nikki, struggling futility against her bonds. At the same time, Sofia leaped, throwing herself at Nikki and toppling the chair.

"*Damien!*" Nikki screamed, and as Breckenridge's shot rang out, Damien stupidly realized that the fall must have knocked the gag loose.

He looked that direction, saw blood, and felt his heart stop.

Then he realized that the blood was Sofia's. She'd jumped on top of Nikki—a human shield—and they'd gone over together.

"Sofia!" He started that direction, then stopped when he saw her pull out the gun. She held it toward him, and in that instant he feared that he really was a dead man.

But then the Glock was sliding across the floor toward him, and Nikki was shouting for him to run.

Breckenridge had recovered from the surprise of Sofia's leap onto Nikki, and now he was aiming for a second shot, this time at Damien, who was sprinting for the gun. He dove for it, then rolled onto his back once the cool metal was in his hands. He couldn't aim—there was no time. He could only hope that the shot would startle Breckenridge enough to knock him off kilter and give Damien time to regroup.

He pulled the trigger, and he fired.

A loud thumping noise filled the room, and for a bizarre moment, he thought it was the sound of the blood spreading around Breckenridge. Then he realized that somehow he'd actually made the shot, right through the bastard's heart.

The man was dead.

The son of a bitch who'd threatened to kill Nikki was actually dead.

And as for the thumping noise—well that was the sound of Ryan's second unit. The team that had been following the Range Rover in a chopper.

As the helicopter landed above them, Damien rushed to Nikki, still strapped to the toppled chair, with Sofia sprawled over her, her white shirt now pink with blood.

"Damien. Oh, God, Damien." Tears streamed down Nikki's face. "She's gone. I'm sorry, but I think she's gone."

He looked down, his heart breaking as he registered Sofia's lifeless form. He looked at Nikki, at Sofia's blood staining her, too.

"She saved me," Nikki said. "That bullet was meant for me."

"I know," he said, the words making him cold. Making him numb.

Behind him, he heard the team crash into the house, Ryan's orders echoing through the rooms.

"I've got you," he whispered to his wife, then gently moved Sofia off her. His hands shook as he untied the ropes that bound her to the chair. And when she was free, she wrapped her arms around him, and he pulled her close. "I knew you'd come," she said. "I knew you'd find me."

"I thought I'd lost you," he said, his words choked with both lingering fear and potent relief. "Baby, I was so terrified that I'd lost you."

"You can't," she said. "We can't lose each other."

He held her tight as she sobbed against him, as his own eyes filled with tears.

He held her as relief finally swept over him, bittersweet from the taint of sorrow.

He held her, simply held her. And he knew that he would never, ever let her go.

Chapter Twenty-eight

The glass case against the back wall held some of his most precious memories. The scrapbook that Nikki had given him, documenting their days and nights together. His signed Ray Bradbury books from the time he'd met the man. The small red folio that held Lara's adoption papers, the words written in Chinese. The bracelet from Anne's wrist identifying her as his child for the hospital.

So many treasures, including his very first award for tennis, earned before the game had become a chore. Before Richter.

Before he'd met Sofia.

And, yes, the case held a photo of her. A small, framed picture of Damien and Sofia and Alaine, laughing together by a lake in Germany. "I remember this day," he said softly, knowing that Nikki had come up behind him.

She pressed a soft hand to his shoulder.

"We'd been happy that day. All three of us."

"Damien."

He turned, then pulled her to him. It had been four days, and miraculously, she was doing fine. "It was horrible," she'd told him the night they'd come home, as they'd held each other in bed, the girls sleeping on either side of them. "And I was so scared. But I knew you'd find me."

"What if I hadn't?"

She'd given him a small, sad smile. "Even if I'd died in there, I would have gone to my death trusting you. Because I know that you would have moved heaven and earth to find me. But you're not a miracle worker. I can only trust the man. And I do, Damien. I trust you completely. I know you'd never give up on me. On the girls."

Then she'd kissed him, and it felt like she was absolving him of all his faults and failures.

And yet still …

"Talk to me," Nikki pressed, taking his hand and tugging him to one of the small couches that dotted the mezzanine, serving as cozy reading nooks.

"What time is it?" He'd tried to sleep, but had given up at least an hour ago. He'd stayed in bed for a while, simply watching Nikki breathe, so thankful that she was there beside him, and still fighting the fear and darkness that lingered from the reality of how close she'd come to being taken from him.

He'd finally gotten up, then gone to the girls' room and pressed gentle kisses to each of their foreheads before coming down here, as if there was some sort of solace he could find in his memories.

"Almost three," she said. "Come back to bed."

"Not yet."

She studied him, then nodded before settling on the couch beside him, still holding his hand. She kissed his fingertips.

"Did I fail her?"

The question had been weighing on him for days.

"Fail her?" Her brow furrowed. "Richter failed her. And Breckenridge killed her. All you've ever done is help her."

"I took her virginity." Grief and self-loathing washed over him.

"And you think that caused this?"

He shuddered. "I took her innocence so that Richter wouldn't. And I killed him—I let him die—so he wouldn't whore her out. I tried to save her. And I wonder if I only made it worse."

"No. You know that's not true. I know you're hurting. But you're not a stupid man, Damien. Don't start acting like one."

He flinched. Her words were harsh, but they were also true.

"I know. I'm feeling sorry for myself. For her, too."

"I get that. But you've spent your whole life helping her. It's not you, it's her. And she broke a long time ago. Maybe she was simply sick, or maybe Richter broke something inside her. Maybe both. But you never harmed her. Just the opposite. You're the reason she had moments of clarity. And maybe that makes it harder, because you saw her potential."

He rubbed his temples, believing her words, but not yet feeling their power.

"Damien, look at me." Her expression, both fierce and loving, captured him. "Sofia would be alive right now if it wasn't for me. We both know it."

He sat perfectly still, and she was right. He couldn't deny it.

"So tell me the truth—do you blame me?"

He flinched, her words hitting him like a physical slap. "What? Nikki, what are you even—"

"Do you blame me?"

"Blame? God, no. Never." He frowned as he focused on her, ignoring everything but the need to make sure Nikki understood that none of it—not one single moment of everything they'd been through— was her fault. Blame her? The idea was absurd. And he told her so.

"I believe you," she said, her voice as soft as a rose petal. "But if you understand that, then you have to know that you can't blame yourself either." She reached out, gripping his upper arms as she earnestly held his gaze.

"It wasn't anyone's fault," she continued. "Not really. It was just inside her. There was darkness there, and she fought it all her life. Sometimes she even battled it back. I think you helped her the most in keeping it down. And the other day, she fought hard enough to save me. And, Damien, she was there to save me because you saved her."

"Do you believe that?"

"Yeah. I do."

"I really have been feeling sorry for myself."

"You need to grieve, I get it. I just don't want you to drown in it."

"I couldn't possibly," he said, tugging her onto his lap. "Not with you around to save me."

Her eyes moved as she studied his face, her lashes damp with tears. "Always," she whispered, and then she kissed him.

And then, surrounded by his memories, he pulled her close, stripped her bare, and made love sweetly and slowly with his wife.

Epilogue

Damien stood barefoot in the surf, watching as the ashes floated on the wind before finally settling on the golden-dappled waves. In the distance, the sun sank toward the horizon, casting the sky in shades of purple and orange. This was Sofia's favorite time of day, and as he put the lid back on the now empty urn, Damien voiced a silent goodbye to his friend.

"She loved you as best she could," Nikki said, her voice as soft as the gentle breeze.

"You always saw her clearly."

"And you saw her through the eyes of love and family. You didn't fail her. She was a screwed-up woman, but she was a lot less screwed up than she would have been if you hadn't been there all those years to help her."

"I know. I do." He kissed her hand. "I know it, and you helped me to believe it, too."

"But?"

He laughed at his wife's perceptiveness. "And yet in so many ways, I was her albatross. Her trigger."

"That's not your fault. You're not Atlas. You don't have to carry the weight of the world on your shoulders."

"I don't," he agreed. "But I do have a very full bank account and connections to a variety of talented people. And I think that it would feel nice to help lighten someone else's burden. To take away some of the fear and give them a little bit of hope."

"This is what you've been talking to Ryan and Quincy about."

"It is."

"And you're serious? A division of Stark Security?"

"You don't like the idea?"

She studied his face, her expression so wide and open and full of love it humbled him. "On the contrary, I can't wait to see what's coming. But right now, will you make love to me?"

"Why?" he asked with a teasing smile, though there was nothing teasing about her answer.

"Because you're a good man."

The words hung for a moment in the air before the wind carried them off over the ocean. He listened to their echo as his wife drew him down to the blanket at their feet. And there, on an empty stretch of beach with the sun sinking below the horizon, he got lost in the arms of the woman he loved.

And he let himself believe her.

* * * *

Also from 1001 Dark Nights and J. Kenner, discover Indulge Me, Hold Me, Tame Me, Tempt Me, Justify Me, Caress of Darkness, Caress of Pleasure, and Rising Storm.

Sign up for the 1001 Dark Nights Newsletter
and be entered to win a Tiffany Lock necklace.

There's a contest every quarter!

Go to www.1001DarkNights.com to subscribe.

As a bonus, all subscribers can download
FIVE FREE exclusive books!

Discover 1001 Dark Nights Collection Six

DRAGON CLAIMED by Donna Grant
A Dark Kings Novella

ASHES TO INK by Carrie Ann Ryan
A Montgomery Ink: Colorado Springs Novella

ENSNARED by Elisabeth Naughton
An Eternal Guardians Novella

EVERMORE by Corinne Michaels
A Salvation Series Novella

VENGEANCE by Rebecca Zanetti
A Dark Protectors/Rebels Novella

ELI'S TRIUMPH by Joanna Wylde
A Reapers MC Novella

CIPHER by Larissa Ione
A Demonica Underworld Novella

RESCUING MACIE by Susan Stoker
A Delta Force Heroes Novella

ENCHANTED by Lexi Blake
A Masters and Mercenaries Novella

TAKE THE BRIDE by Carly Phillips
A Knight Brothers Novella

INDULGE ME by J. Kenner
A Stark Ever After Novella

THE KING by Jennifer L. Armentrout
A Wicked Novella

QUIET MAN by Kristen Ashley
A Dream Man Novella

ABANDON by Rachel Van Dyken
A Seaside Pictures Novella

THE OPEN DOOR by Laurelin Paige
A Found Duet Novella

CLOSER by Kylie Scott
A Stage Dive Novella

SOMETHING JUST LIKE THIS by Jennifer Probst
A Stay Novella

BLOOD NIGHT by Heather Graham
A Krewe of Hunters Novella

TWIST OF FATE by Jill Shalvis
A Heartbreaker Bay Novella

MORE THAN PLEASURE YOU by Shayla Black
A More Than Words Novella

WONDER WITH ME by Kristen Proby
A With Me In Seattle Novella

THE DARKEST ASSASSIN by Gena Showalter
A Lords of the Underworld Novella

About J. Kenner

J. Kenner (aka Julie Kenner) is the *New York Times, USA Today, Publishers Weekly, Wall Street Journal* and #1 International bestselling author of over one-hundred novels, novellas and short stories in a variety of genres.

JK has been praised by *Publishers Weekly* as an author with a "flair for dialogue and eccentric characterizations" and by *RT Bookclub* for having "cornered the market on sinfully attractive, dominant antiheroes and the women who swoon for them." A six-time finalist for Romance Writers of America's prestigious RITA award, JK took home the first RITA trophy awarded in the category of erotic romance in 2014 for her novel, *Claim Me* (book 2 of her Stark Saga) and in 2018 for her novel Wicked Dirty.

In her previous career as an attorney, JK worked as a lawyer in Southern California and Texas. She currently lives in Central Texas, with her husband, two daughters, and two rather spastic cats.

Visit JK online at www.jkenner.com
Subscribe to JK's Newsletter
Text JKenner to 21000 to subscribe to JK's text alerts
Twitter
Instagram
Facebook Page
Facebook Fan Group

Discover More J. Kenner/Julie Kenner

Indulge Me: A Stark Ever After Novella by J. Kenner
Coming July 9, 2019

Despite everything I have suffered, I never truly understood darkness until my family was in danger. Those desperate hours came close to breaking both Damien and me, but together we found the strength to survive and hold our family together.

Even so, my wounds are deep, and wispy shadows still linger. But Damien is my rock. My hero against the dark and violence.

And when dark memories threaten to consume me, he whisks me away, knowing that in order to conquer my fears he must take control. Demand my submission. Claim me completely. Because if I am going to find my center again, I must hold tight to Damien and draw deep from the wellspring of our shared passion.

* * * *

Hold Me: A Stark Ever After Novella by Julie Kenner
Now Available

My life with Damien has never been fuller. Every day is a miracle, and every night I lose myself in the oasis of his arms.

But there are new challenges, too. Our families. Our careers. And new responsibilities that test us with unrelenting, unexpected trials.

I know we will survive—we have to. Because I cannot live without Damien by my side. But sometimes the darkness seems overwhelming, and I am terrified that the day will come when Damien cannot bring the light. And I will have to find the strength inside myself to find my way back into his arms.

* * * *

Justify Me: A Stark International/Masters and Mercenaries Novella by J. Kenner

McKay-Taggart operative Riley Blade has no intention of returning to Los Angeles after his brief stint as a consultant on mega-star Lyle Tarpin's latest action flick. Not even for Natasha Black, Tarpin's sexy personal assistant who'd gotten under his skin. Why would he, when Tasha made it absolutely clear that—attraction or not—she wasn't interested in a fling, much less a relationship.

But when Riley learns that someone is stalking her, he races to her side. Determined to not only protect her, but to convince her that—no matter what has hurt her in the past—he's not only going to fight for her, he's going to win her heart. Forever.

* * * *

Tame Me: A Stark International Novella by J. Kenner
Now Available

Aspiring actress Jamie Archer is on the run. From herself. From her wild child ways. From the screwed up life that she left behind in Los Angeles. And, most of all, from Ryan Hunter—the first man who has the potential to break through her defenses to see the dark fears and secrets she hides.

Stark International Security Chief Ryan Hunter knows only one thing for sure—he wants Jamie. Wants to hold her, make love to her, possess her, and claim her. Wants to do whatever it takes to make her his.

But after one night of bliss, Jamie bolts. And now it's up to Ryan to not only bring her back, but to convince her that she's running away from the best thing that ever happened to her--him.

* * * *

Tempt Me: A Stark International Novella by J. Kenner
Now Available

Sometimes passion has a price...

When sexy Stark Security Chief Ryan Hunter whisks his girlfriend Jamie Archer away for a passionate, romance-filled weekend so he can finally pop the question, he's certain that the answer will be an enthusiastic yes. So when Jamie tries to avoid the conversation, hiding her fears of commitment and change under a blanket of wild sensuality and decadent playtime in bed, Ryan is more determined than ever to convince Jamie that they belong together.

Knowing there's no halfway with this woman, Ryan gives her an ultimatum – marry him or walk away. Now Jamie is forced to face her deepest insecurities or risk destroying the best thing in her life. And it will take all of her strength, and all of Ryan's love, to keep her right where she belongs...

* * * *

Caress of Darkness: A Dark Pleasures Novella by Julie Kenner
Now Available

From the first moment I saw him, I knew that Rainer Engel was like no other man. Dangerously sexy and darkly mysterious, he both enticed me and terrified me.

I wanted to run–to fight against the heat that was building between us–but there was nowhere to go. I needed his help as much as I needed his touch. And so help me, I knew that I would do anything he asked in order to have both.

But even as our passion burned hot, the secrets in Raine's past reached out to destroy us ... and we would both have to make the greatest sacrifice to find a love that would last forever.

Don't miss the next novellas in the Dark Pleasures series!

Find Me in Darkness, Find Me in Pleasure, Find Me in Passion, Caress of Pleasure…

* * * *

Storm, Texas.

Where passion runs hot, desire runs deep, and secrets have the power to destroy…

Nestled among rolling hills and painted with vibrant wildflowers, the bucolic town of Storm, Texas, seems like nothing short of perfection.

But there are secrets beneath the facade. Dark secrets. Powerful secrets. The kind that can destroy lives and tear families apart. The kind that can cut through a town like a tempest, leaving jealousy and destruction in its wake, along with shattered hopes and broken dreams. All it takes is one little thing to shatter that polish.

Rising Storm is a series conceived by Julie Kenner and Dee Davis to read like an on-going drama. Set in a small Texas town, Rising Storm is full of scandal, deceit, romance, passion, and secrets. Lots of secrets.

Shattered With You
Stark Security Book 1
By J. Kenner
Coming March 26, 2019

Charismatic. Dangerous. Sexy as hell.

Meet the men of Stark Security.

Stark Security, a high-end, high-tech, no-holds barred security firm founded by billionaire Damien Stark and security specialist Ryan Hunter has one mission: Do whatever it takes to protect the innocent. Only the best in the business are good enough for Stark Security.

Men with dangerous skills.

Men with something to prove.

Brilliant, charismatic, sexy as hell, they have no time for softness—they work hard and they play harder. They'll take any risk to get the job done.

But what they won't do is lose their hearts.

On behalf of 1001 Dark Nights,
Liz Berry and M.J. Rose would like to thank ~

Steve Berry
Doug Scofield
Kim Guidroz
Jillian Stein
InkSlinger PR
Dan Slater
Asha Hossain
Chris Graham
Fedora Chen
Kasi Alexander
Jessica Johns
Dylan Stockton
Richard Blake
and Simon Lipskar

Made in the USA
Monee, IL
08 August 2021